For more than forty years,
Yearling has been the leading name
in classic and award-winning literature
for young readers.

Yearling books feature children's
favorite authors and characters,
providing dynamic stories of adventure,
humor, history, mystery, and fantasy.

Trust Yearling paperbacks to entertain,
inspire, and promote the love of reading
in all children.

OTHER YEARLING BOOKS YOU WILL ENJOY

The Daring
Adventures of
Penhaligon
Brush

A YEARLING BOOK

Published by Yearling, an imprint of Random House Children's Books
a division of Random House, Inc., New York

This is a work of fiction. Names, characters, places, and incidents either are the product of the
author's imagination or are used fictitiously. Any resemblance to actual persons, living or dead, events,
or locales is entirely coincidental.

Text copyright © 2007 by S. Jones Rogan
Illustrations copyright © 2007 by Christian Slade

Visit us on the Web! www.randomhouse.com/kids

Educators and librarians, for a variety of teaching tools, visit us at www.randomhouse.com/teachers

The Library of Congress has cataloged the hardcover edition of this work as follows:

Rogan, S. Jones (Sally Jones)
The daring adventures of Penhaligon Brush / by S. Jones Rogan ; Christian Slade.
p. cm.
Summary: When Penhaligon Brush the fox is summoned by his step-brother to the seaside town of
Porthleven, he finds immediately upon arrival that his brother is incarcerated in the dungeon at
Ferball Manor.
ISBN: 978-0-375-84344-0 (trade)—ISBN: 978-0-375-94344-7 (lib. bdg.)
[1. Foxes—Fiction. 2. Animals—Fiction. 3. Adventure and adventurers—Fiction.]
I. Slade, Christian, ill. II. Title.
PZ7.R625525Dar 2007
[Fic]—dc22
2006035566

ISBN: 978-0-440-42208-2 (pbk.)

Reprinted by arrangement with Alfred A. Knopf Books for Young Readers

Printed in the United States of America

April 2009

10 9 8 7 6 5 4 3 2 1

First Yearling Edition

To Dad, who loved Porthleven
—S.J.R.

To Mom & Dad
—C.S.

# Contents

To Penzance

Rock Pool Beach

Ferball Manor

Porthleven

Brigand's
Point

Sandy Cove

N

W        E

S

Sheepwash

River Ramble

Ramble-on-the-Water

The Moor

Falmouth

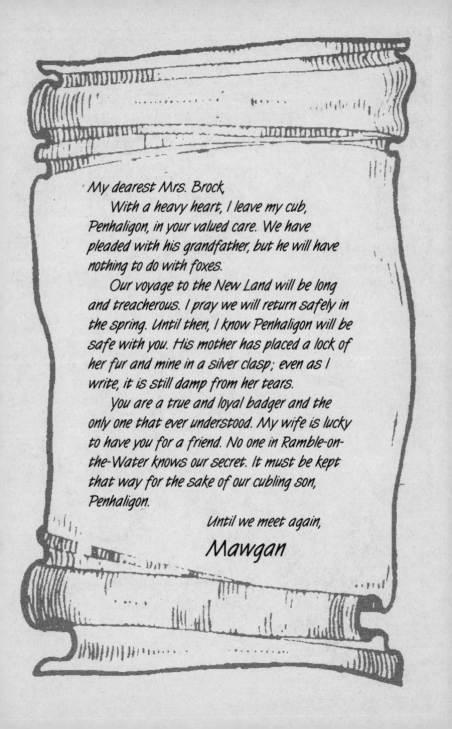

My dearest Mrs. Brock,

With a heavy heart, I leave my cub, Penhaligon, in your valued care. We have pleaded with his grandfather, but he will have nothing to do with foxes.

Our voyage to the New Land will be long and treacherous. I pray we will return safely in the spring. Until then, I know Penhaligon will be safe with you. His mother has placed a lock of her fur and mine in a silver clasp; even as I write, it is still damp from her tears.

You are a true and loyal badger and the only one that ever understood. My wife is lucky to have you for a friend. No one in Ramble-on-the-Water knows our secret. It must be kept that way for the sake of our cubling son, Penhaligon.

Until we meet again,

Mawgan

# Some Things Never Change

## CHAPTER ONE

"It'll never come off, you know," Bill Goat said carelessly as Penhaligon Brush polished the sign on the apothecary door. Today, it seemed, was to be the same as every other day; the nasty black mark on the sign refused to budge. It was etched into the brass, just above the apostrophe *S*, where it was written:

*PENHALIGON'S APOTHECARY*
*CURES FOR ALL KNOWN ILLS*

Penhaligon rubbed harder. The door rattled on its hinges. The fox's rust-colored tail swished angrily, knocking over his basket of polishes. "Flaming foxgloves," he muttered, dabbing his furry brow with the polishing cloth.

Bill Goat, leaning on his walking stick, had been watching Penhaligon's lack of progress for some time. "You've been polishing that sign every morning since old Menhenin died." He pulled thoughtfully at his white beard. "Almost six seasons now."

Penhaligon's ears twitched. "Five and one-half," he said, throwing down the cloth at the polish tin.

"He was a strange fox, that Menhenin," said Bill. "The way he wore them long robes and funny hats like some mysterious foreigner."

"Turbans," muttered Penhaligon.

"Speaking of foreigners, d'you hear the crown prince is marrying a creature from Spatavia? I've never even heard of Spatavia. Must be quite exciting, marrying someone from Spatavia."

Penhaligon grunted, gathering his polishing tools. Excitement was something he'd forgotten about long ago.

"Wonderful with the cures, though."

"Spatavians?" asked Penhaligon.

"Bah! No, Menhenin," said Bill Goat. "Mrs. Goat was a martyr to her rheumatism till he gave her the medicinal salve. Which reminds me why I'm here. She needs more drops for her earache." The old goat glanced at the school clock tower across the street. It was almost eight-thirty. "You *will* be opening this morning, I suppose?"

Penhaligon sighed. "Same time as usual, Bill. I'll have a bottle of ear drops ready by lunchtime. I'll bring them with me to the Warren Arms. I expect you'll be there for lunch as usual?"

"Very obliging, I'm sure," said Bill.

Penhaligon scratched at the black mark with his claw.

The goat hobbled up the street, but he called back over his shoulder, "I'd learn to live with that mark if I were you. Some things you just can't change."

Bill's words rang in Penhaligon's ears. "I know," he sighed. He was still a young fox, but sometimes he felt so responsible, so dull, so . . . old.

Penhaligon turned his attention to the scarlet geraniums growing cheerily in the window boxes. He smiled. When he was a cub, he'd dreamed of adventure on the high seas. He would sail the world in search of his parents, whom he'd never known.

"They've been captured by a pirate king," he'd announce to Mrs. Brock, the kindly badger who had taken him in. "I'll help them to escape, and we'll all be home in time for tea." But they never "escaped."

Mrs. Brock would bury Penhaligon's tear-stained

snout in her large apron and stroke his ears. She never did tell him what had happened to his parents. He wasn't sure she even knew. And so it remained a mystery.

Penhaligon snorted. The mark on the brass sign had the better of him as usual, and he wasn't a cub anymore. He now had different ideas why his parents had abandoned him. He pinched off a dead geranium flower.

Scooping up his basket and nodding a good-morning to a couple of squirrel villagers, Penhaligon disappeared inside his shop.

From floor to ceiling, old wooden shelves lined the walls. They were crammed with hundreds of glass bottles of all shapes and sizes: pills and powders, syrups and salves, herbals and healing plasters, all neatly labeled and placed alphabetically in order of ailment. Penhaligon raised the blinds.

The bottles, shot with sunlight, flashed like precious stones: rubies, sapphires, opals, and amethysts. The long marble counter was set with glass measures and brass scales, implements for cutting and chopping, mixing and mashing. A wooden chair with a well-worn seat was placed behind.

He removed his tweed jacket and folded it neatly across the back of the chair. It was another warm day.

His coarse fur was tipped unusually darker than most foxes', and he preferred cool weather so he could keep his jacket on.

"You would have been extremely hot and uncomfortable today," Penhaligon told the huge oil portrait of Menhenin, whose beady eyes stared from his silk-swathed, turbaned head.

Bill Goat was right. The old fox had insisted on wearing the bizarre garments sent to him by a grateful Uvian prince, or so he told Penhaligon.

The painting of Menhenin watched silently as the fox rolled up his crisp white shirtsleeves. He set about preparing the day's cures, starting with Mrs. Goat's ear drops.

Penhaligon had worked hard to take Menhenin's place, proud to inherit the important role of Ramble-on-the-Water's apothecary, caring for the sick. Most of the villagers had their doubts. "Too young a fox to take on such responsibility," they said.

It was true he hadn't fully finished his apprenticeship before Menhenin had died of a fever that neither of them could cure. But Penhaligon was sharp and had a natural talent. If there was an unfamiliar ailment, he would scour Menhenin's apothecary books. Soon his remedies were trusted and sought after even as far away as the Moor. The edge of the Moor, that is, for no civilized creature lived upon the Moor, only the wild Romany wolves.

As Penhaligon measured and mixed, he wondered if the villagers had been right. What had he seen? What had he done?

He'd visited Bancroft Brock, his badger brother, a couple of times. But then Porthleven, the small, sleepy fishing village where Bancroft was schoolmaster, was hardly a hub of excitement and adventure. The last visit had been when Mrs. Brock had finally lived out her seasons. Poor Mrs. Brock. What would he have done without her?

He sighed, took down a jar, and measured an exact amount of chamomile powder into a stone mortar. He ground the powder with a heavy pestle, then added buttercup cream. He knew exactly what was in each one of his bottles, just as he knew exactly what would happen today. Gertrude, his bubbly assistant, would come to work. "Good morning," she'd say. It was Wednesday, so he'd leave early and go to the Warren Arms for lunch, the same as every other Wednesday. Penhaligon scratched his ears and yawned.

The shop door opened and a chubby young fox walked in. "Good morning," she said.

"Good morning, Gertrude," Penhaligon said with a sigh.

"Anything wrong?" Gertrude looked concerned.

"Nothing's wrong, Gertrude. Everything's right; that's the problem."

Gertrude, puzzled, blinked her large brown eyes.

"Here," he said, patting her on the shoulder. "Finish mixing this chamomile salve for young Barnaby Batwing's sunburn." Penhaligon took down a jar filled with lemon drops. He scooped some into a bag. "Send him these too."

"No wonder you're so popular with the young ones," said Gertrude with a giggle.

Menhenin had taught Penhaligon to make boiled-sugar cough drops when he was a schoolcub. Now he concocted all kinds of delicious flavors.

"I think I'll go for a walk before lunch, Gertrude." He pasted a label, FOR GOATS' EARS ONLY, on a small blue bottle and grabbed his jacket.

Gertrude nodded eagerly. Penhaligon knew she loved to be left in charge of the shop. She was a very bright apprentice and had been blessed with the gift of curing. He'd spotted it in her just as Menhenin had seen it in him years ago.

The sun warmed his shoulders as he headed up

Cowslip Lane to the Warren Arms. The village green was quiet as usual, except for the gurgling waters of the River Ramble that cut through its center.

Life in Ramble-on-the-Water was always quiet. And there was time, plenty of time; Penhaligon had already finished reading two books that week. There was time for long hikes to collect plant ingredients for his pills and potions. Time to fish in the River Ramble. Time for boredom.

It was still too early for lunch, so Penhaligon found a grassy spot by the river. He might have studied the clouds and noticed how the water ran clear as crystal, but soft little snores quivered the edges of his snout.

He never could have imagined that this would be his last nap on the banks of the River Ramble for a very, very long time.

# The Adventure Begins

## CHAPTER TWO

S ome time later, Penhaligon sat in his regular
window seat in the Warren Arms sipping his
usual pint of blackberry ale. He had given Mrs.
Goat's ear drops to Bill and was deciding whether or
not to go fishing that afternoon, vaguely aware of the
other customers chattering about the Spatavian princess their crown prince was to marry. Cuthbert Ramsbottom, the landlord, fingered the large gold hoop in
his left horn.

"This is Spatavian gold," he boomed proudly. "It's
the best there is. Look at the lettering, right there . . .
SPATAVIA, that says."

There was a murmur of approval from his customers.

"That reminds me." Cuthbert took down the letter he'd placed on his DON'T FORGET shelf. "I say, Mr.

Penhaligon," he announced. "I forgot, there's a letter here for ye."

Penhaligon recognized the hand at once. It was from Bancroft Brock. He opened it carefully.

> My dear Penhaligon,
>   I have important news, too complicated to write in a letter. You must come to Porthleven immediately. Look for me in the Cat and Fiddle.
>                    Your friend and brother,
>                    **Bancroft**
> P.S. Hurry up.

Penhaligon folded the letter and placed it in his waistcoat pocket. It was most unlike Bancroft to summon him at a moment's notice. His news must truly be important. Strangely, there was no date on the letter.

Penhaligon decided he should leave immediately. But how could he? The village depended on him. What if there was an outbreak of some terrible disease and he wasn't here to help? Penhaligon tried to remember when there was a terrible outbreak of anything in Ramble-on-the-Water. Gertrude was very capable and could look after things for a short time. It would certainly be good to see Bancroft again.

He stared thoughtfully into his glass, and just as he was about to take a sip, his ale started to vibrate and slosh around. "What the . . . ?" A loud clatter rooted him to his seat.

*Thrump-thrump-thrump. Thrump-thrumpity-thrump.* The ale pots and tankards jumped on their shelves behind the bar.

"Whatever is that noise, Cuthbert?"

"By the Romany wolves, I dunno, I'm sure, sir." Cuthbert's deep voice quivered. "Never 'eard nothing like it before."

The windowpanes jiggled in their frames. Penhaligon set his drink down, and the glass walked its way to the table's edge.

As the strange noise approached the Warren Arms, another sound joined in, a sort of *clack-clack, clack-clack* clanking of metal. Cuthbert tried to stop the hanging tankards from swaying off their hooks. Penhaligon and the other customers crowded to the window. What manner of monster could possibly cause such a chaotic din? They soon found out.

Raising clouds of dust as they went, a troop of the king's Warthog Army marched along the highway. Their

helmets glinted in the sun. Their tusks were thrust proudly forward. And although their scarlet-and-gold uniforms were covered in dust, they were an impressive sight.

"Would you look at that," said Cuthbert. "Where are they off to?"

"Falmouth," said a small, stoatish-looking creature. "I've just traveled from there. Princess Katrina's sailing ships arrive this week from Spatavia. The whole town is decorated like a Uvian palace at Micklemas."

Bill Goat tugged his beard. "I heard there's dowry of enough gold and jeweled brocade on her ship to turn a saint to villainy. They'll be going to guard the treasure, you can be sure."

The inhabitants of the Warren Arms watched the seemingly endless line of soldiers march by.

"Look, it's Crown Prince Tamar himself," shouted someone.

"Let me see! Let me see!" bleated Bill Goat. "I've never seen a royal before." The handsome face of a feline was just visible through his helmet visor. Everyone gasped and pointed.

The noisy clatter finally trickled into the distance; Ramble-on-the-Water was quiet once more. Everyone returned to their seats, chattering excitedly.

"Shame he couldn't 'ave stopped for a pint of my famous ale," said Cuthbert Ramsbottom, straightening a couple of pictures. "The landlords in Falmouth will be right busy with that lot in town. Wish I could be there to join them. Never been farther than the edge of the Moor before."

"What a wonderful idea," Penhaligon mumbled to

himself. Falmouth was only a short distance from Porthleven. Perhaps he and Bancroft could deal with Bancroft's important business, then join the festivities in Falmouth. They'd watch the Spatavian ships come in with their tall masts and full sails.

He returned his empty glass to the bar. "Well, Cuthbert," he said, "this is my last pint of your excellent blackberry ale for a while. I'm off to see Bancroft."

"Bit sudden, Mr. Penhaligon, isn't it? Everything all right?"

"Cuthbert, everything is always all right in Porthleven. Flowers bloom at every cottage window. The bright-painted fishing boats always catch the tastiest fish. The sun always seems to shine. Everyone is happy and friendly."

"Shame Mrs. Brock's seasons came to an end recently. You both must miss her," said Cuthbert.

Penhaligon felt his throat tighten. He brushed back his ears and nodded.

Bill Goat, who'd been listening as usual, joined the conversation. "Give Bancroft our regards," he said. "We miss his Friday-night storytellin'." All the customers murmured their agreement. "Mrs. Goat says Friday nights have never been the same."

"I'll be sure to pass on the messages." With a wave, Penhaligon marched into the street, where little swirls of dust from the Warthog Army still hung in the air.

🐾 🐾 🐾 🐾

Penhaligon rummaged through drawers and cupboards until he found his canvas knapsack. He knew exactly what to pack. He'd often thought about what he would pack should he be called off at a moment's notice, and finally that time had come. He placed two clean shirts, an extra pair of britches, and a furbrush into the knapsack. In the side pockets he slipped his toothbrush, a salve for stings and rashes, one or two herbal powders for emergencies, and a handkerchief. He dropped a homemade honey-apple bar and a few coins into his pocket. He wouldn't need any other food; Bancroft loved to cook, and there was sure to be a steaming pot of stew and freshly baked bread waiting for him.

He checked his image in the hall mirror, smoothing the rather coarse fur under his bright brown eyes. Yes, he looked like a fox befitting his station: smartly dressed, well groomed, about to embark on his travels.

Gertrude had already left for Barnaby Batwing's house, so he tacked a note on the apothecary door:

*Dear Gertrude,*
*Had to visit Bancroft on important business.*
*Please look after everything for a few days.*
*See you when I return.*

# Penhaligon

*P.S. Please water my geraniums. Thanks.*
*P.P.S. Don't forget to polish the sign.*

There was no one on the village green as Penhaligon made his way to the tree-lined highway. With luck he would hitch a fast ride and be at Porthleven by nightfall.

🕯 🕯 🕯 🕯

The late-afternoon sun cast Penhaligon's shadow across the road as he sat, waiting. Not a cart or a coach had passed by. "This is not a good start to my travels," he muttered, unbuttoning his tweed jacket.

On the far side of the village the clock tower on top of the school struck four bells. The sound reminded him of his not so happy days at that very school. The other pupils would tease him cruelly.

"Your foxy fur's tipped so dark your mama thought you were a badger," they'd taunt. Or worse: "Poor

Foxy Brock, his mama and papa got eaten by the Romany wolves."

The thought of his parents being a meal for the legendary savage wolves from the Moor was too much to bear. Penhaligon's soft brown eyes would fill with tears. The bullies would snigger and laugh . . . until Bancroft, who was a large badger, even then, arrived.

"Leave my brother alone," he'd shout, sharp claws bared. There was many a scrap in the schoolyard. Mrs. Brock despaired when the two arrived home with bloody snouts.

Penhaligon would ask again, "Did the Romany wolves really eat my parents?"

Mrs. Brock would hug him, tears in her eyes. "Course not, m'darlin'," she'd say.

"Then where are they?" he'd sob.

As the years passed, he stopped asking. It seemed to upset the old badger as much as it did him. But deep down, in the quiet of his soul, Penhaligon felt that the Romany wolves did indeed have something to do with his parents' disappearance.

Still, school was a long time ago. Who cared if he was adopted? Who cared if his ears were larger and his fur was coarse and longer than that of most other foxes round about?

Just then, he
heard rumbling
wheels and some
creature's untuneful
singing. A cart piled
high with wheat sheaves
trundled into view. A very
rotund pig-boar farmer
was trying to sing a high
note in "Nymphs and
Shepherds, Come Away."

Penhaligon sprang into
action. He was taking no
chances that the farmer should
refuse him a ride.

He scrambled up a large oak tree and sidled along a strong limb that stretched over the road. The cart was so slow he could have had another lunch while he waited hidden in the leaves. Finally, the cart beneath him, Penhaligon leaped from his branch.

# A Ghost Town

## CHAPTER THREE

T he farmer, still singing loudly, never heard the thud as the fox landed in the cart.

"Come away, come away, nyyy-mphth and she-heh-pudth," he boomed with a lisp. Penhaligon covered his ears.

"He hasn't stopped for the last three miles," shouted a squeaky voice.

Penhaligon turned to see a mouse with a wheat grain stuck in each ear. He looked miserable.

"That's unfortunate," replied Penhaligon. "Maybe he'll get thirsty soon; it's very warm."

They were both relieved when, at last, loud snores came from the farmer's mouth instead of singing. The horse plodded, weaving along the general direction of the road. Now that they had left the forest behind, Penhaligon could see for miles over the rolling countryside.

Far away to the south was the purple Moor, the

place where the Romany wolves roamed, looking for unsuspecting creatures unfortunate enough to blunder into their domain.

When he was a young cub, Penhaligon was fascinated by schoolyard tales of the wild creatures—howls in the night and stolen youngsters, only the ones who didn't behave of course. Mrs. Brock had a habit of changing the subject whenever Penhaligon asked about such things, and Menhenin would tell him to concentrate on his studies instead of listening to gossip. To this day Penhaligon had never seen a Romany wolf, and they remained a mystery he was happy not to solve.

"Are you traveling far?" asked the mouse.

"To Porthleven to see my brother, Bancroft. And where might you be traveling to?" asked Penhaligon politely.

"I'll be jumping off at the next crossroads. My sister and her family live around here. She's just had another eight newborns." The mouse patted a large carpetbag by his side. "It's tough on birthdays and Micklemas."

"I should think so," said Penhaligon, raising eyebrows at the strings of pink and blue ribbon spilling from the bulging bag. The mouse continued to chatter away about his family. Penhaligon would have liked to nap, but instead he nodded politely when appropriate until the mouse mentioned that his sister had been feeling unwell of late.

"I expect the poor thing is thoroughly overtired," said Penhaligon. "Tell her to take plenty of strawberry-and-nettle tea and try to put her paws up in the afternoon."

"Thanks," said the mouse. "I'll tell her. Well, this is me," he squeaked as he shoved his bag over the side. There was a crash of something breaking. The mouse shrugged. "Happens every time. Nice to meet you. Have a lovely time at the seaside," he shouted, and leaped from the cart, rolling like a furry ball along the road until he hit a patch of dandelion clocks.

Penhaligon was not sure how far the turnoff for Porthleven would be. He played eye-spy with himself, but that wasn't much fun. Wrens chirped above him, the wheat smell soothed his senses, the rumbling cart rocked gently, and, wrapped up in sunshine, he fell asleep.

🕯 🕯 🕯 🕯

Stars dotted the indigo sky when Penhaligon awoke. The pig-boar farmer had cloaked himself against the chilly night, and Penhaligon could see only the top of his head nodding gently, fast asleep.

The fox hadn't any idea where they were or even if the cart was heading in the right direction. How long had he been asleep? Presently they reached a crossroads. Penhaligon read the signpost by the full moon's light:

SHEEPWASH ½ MILE

PORTHLEVEN 2 MILES

The Porthleven sign was pointing back the way they'd come. "Flaming foxgloves," said Penhaligon. "We've gone too far."

"Who thed that?" asked the lisping farmer, turning this way and that.

"Thanks for the ride," Penhaligon told the startled pig-boar farmer as he slid from the cart.

He hurried the distance back to the turnoff, hoping that Bancroft's supper would not be spoiled by the time he arrived. At last he started down the steep, narrow lane to Porthleven. He could smell the salty sea already. The air felt damp and clinging. He knew that behind the tall hedgerows, the meadows rolled down to the cliffs where the ocean would be sparkling in the moonlight.

The hedgerows towered overhead, forming an eerie tunnel. Penhaligon's lonely footsteps echoed through his empty stomach and up to his ears. He flinched as an owl hooted from somewhere in the darkness.

Penhaligon walked a little faster. Visions popped uninvited into his head as he remembered Bancroft's fireside tales of fearsome smugglers and hangman gibbets. Strange shadows seemed to grow from the overhanging trees.

"Not far now," he muttered to himself as cheerily as he could muster.

The lane became steeper. "Strange," murmured Penhaligon. "I should see the lights of the village by now."

An inky blackness was all there was. He stood still, waiting to see the warning beam from the lighthouse sweep across Porthleven Bay. There was nothing. "That's impossible. The lighthouse lamp is always shining." Penhaligon felt the roots of his fur tingle.

Rumbling clouds gathered over the stars, and a large plop of rain fell on his snout. Penhaligon turned up his collar. Rain was the one thing he'd not come prepared for. The breeze picked up. The bushes around him rustled, reaching for him with an uncanny life of their own. "It's just the wind," he told himself. "I know it's just the wind."

Lightning flashed through the sky. Penhaligon caught sight of Porthleven at the bottom of the hill. It looked as lifeless as a grave.

He stood for a second to wipe the rain from his eyes. A crack of thunder pierced his ears. Penhaligon's heart froze.

A hunched figure covered with long, slimy hair blocked his path. He stared at the thing. The thing stared back with burning yellow eyes. Penhaligon let out a yelp. But in the next flash of lightning, it was gone.

He sprinted the rest of the way to the village, not daring to look behind him, not noticing the peeling paint of the cottages or the dead flowers in their window boxes. He ran through the darkened streets, stopping only when he was quite sure he'd left the thing behind.

"Someone is playing a prank," he gasped to himself. "When I get to the Cat and Fiddle, they'll tell me what's going on."

The rain clouds passed, and the moon now lit Penhaligon's way to the harbor. The narrow street opened into the wide cobblestoned quayside, beyond which

the fishing boats bobbed up and down. A shivery breeze plucked through the rigging, twanging like the sinews on a dead creature's bones.

On the far side of the quay was the Cat and Fiddle public house, a place filled with raucous laughter and merry souls last time Penhaligon was here. Now it was locked and barred. Dark windows stared like empty sockets.

"It's not possible. There has to be someone there." The fox ran as though his life depended on it. He dodged through the torn fishermen's nets that swayed on their frames like ghostly webs. He leaped over lobster pots, rotten, mildewed, and strewn along the dock. He passed the fishing boats, paint peeling and boards rotting, as they floated in the murky water.

Penhaligon banged on the door of the Cat and Fiddle. He knocked again and again, desperate. Bancroft was not there. Not one of the friendly folk of Porthleven came to his aid. He sank on his haunches, breathless, soaked, and hungry. "It must be a plague," he thought aloud. "Don't be ridiculous," he answered himself. "Bancroft would have told me if there was a plague."

A strange smell invaded Penhaligon's snout. It wasn't the salty sea spray, and it wasn't the odor of fish. He walked to the edge of the quay, the puddles sloshing over the tops of his once-shiny polished boots. He looked into the harbor, wiping his dripping fur from his eyes.

"Flaming foxgloves! The water's covered in stinking black tar."

"Aye, it is," said a raspy voice.

Penhaligon whirled round to see a hedgehog, barely recognizable under a huge sou'wester, save for a few spines sticking out of the collar of his oilskins.

"What's happened around here?" asked Penhaligon. "Where is everybody? Where's Bancroft?"

"Bancroft?" repeated the hedgehog. "Bancroft Brock, the schoolteacher?"

Penhaligon nodded. "Do you know where he is?"

"Can't talk 'ere," said the hedgehog. "The guard will be searching for curfew breakers."

Penhaligon was just about to ask, "What guard? What curfew?" when the clock tower chimed the quarter hour. The slow, muffled beat of a drum echoed around the quayside.

*Thrump, thrump, thrump, thrump.* The hairs on

Penhaligon's back started to prickle. The eerie sound was coming toward them.

"Quick, follow me." The hedgehog scurried across the quay and started up a hilly street. Penhaligon, not wishing to find out who, or rather, *what* was beating the drum, hurried after.

# Hotchi's Bad News

## CHAPTER FOUR

By the time Penhaligon caught up, the hedgehog had ducked into the narrow alleyways of fishermen's cottages. Darting this way and that, he finally slipped inside a door of a whitewashed cottage. Penhaligon followed.

The room was dimly lit. Apart from a table and chairs, a pipe rack, and a corner full of heaped straw, the room was bare. A mother hedgehog and her three hoglets huddled around a sparse fire in the grate.

"Why all the creeping around?" asked Penhaligon. "Porthleven seems to have changed since I was last here."

"You're not wrong, my friend." The hedgehog growled. "Things 'ave changed and not for the better. As for your friend, Bancroft, well, I'm afraid you be too late to save 'im."

Penhaligon's empty stomach lurched when he

heard the words. "Save him?" he demanded. "What do you mean, save him?"

"He's been arrested. He's locked in the dungeon at Ferball Manor," said the hedgehog.

"There's been some mistake. Arrested? That's ridiculous. Why was he arrested? Bancroft would never break the law," said Penhaligon.

"Shh!" The hedgehog lowered his eyes. "They'll hear you . . . that's if they don't smell you first."

The ghoulish drumbeat had caught up with them and resounded through the alley outside. Louder and louder . . . *thrump-thrump, thrump-thrump, thrump-thrump.*

Penhaligon swallowed hard. "Do you think they saw us?" he whispered.

"Pray they did not," answered the hedgehog. The little hoglets drew in tight against their mother. Ghostly shadows cast grotesque shapes across the window. The drumbeat stopped.

Loud sniffs filtered through the cracks around the cottage door, up, down, top, and bottom. The hedgehog put his finger to his mouth. The hoglets squeezed their eyes closed. Penhaligon willed his heart to stop beating so loud. A chill of evil seemed to seep through the cracks as the sniffers continued for several long seconds. They know I'm here, thought Penhaligon, his heart pounding wildly. He waited for the door to burst open.

Finally, the drum sounded again. The menacing beat moved slowly away. When the drum was quite distant, the hedgehogs sighed with relief.

"The name's Hotchi." The hedgehog extended a paw. "Hotchi-witchi. I don't know how you walked past the guard post on the hill, but you'd better escape Porthleven before they know you're here. They have a very keen sense of smell, especially for strangers. And extra specially since Bancroft was, I mean is, a friend of yours."

"My name's Penhaligon Brush, from Ramble-on-the-Water. Tell me, Hotchi, just who exactly are 'they,' and when did this all start? I received a letter from Bancroft just this morning. It doesn't make sense."

"Well, it's been weeks now, I s'pose, since Lady Ferball's nephew arrived in Porthleven." Hotchi reached for a clay pipe from the rack over the fireplace. He patted his hoglets' heads. Penhaligon noticed how thin they looked, for all their spines. "He came from somewhere up north when Lady Ferball got sick. Said he'd take over her affairs for 'er till she got better. He used

to come here when he was a youngster, some say." Hotchi grunted. "I don't remember him, mind. So he says he'll help manage the lands and the tenants—that's us here in Porthleven. Well, he's managed us all right." Hotchi smashed his pipe down onto the table. "He's managed us good and proper, he 'as, and Lady Ferball ain't got no better. First, it were pneumonia, but now she ain't right in the head, they say."

Hotchi looked at the broken pieces of pipe; a tear appeared in his eye. The oldest hoglet hugged him hard. "Don't worry, Papa," she said. "Mr. Brush will help us, won't you?"

"Ah, my brave little one," said Hotchi. "Do you know, Mr. Brush, sir, my little Hannah managed to steal a whole loaf of bread right from under the nose of the guard last week?"

Penhaligon raised his eyebrows.

"Oh, I know what you're thinking," said Hotchi. "But it's stealing or starving around here."

Hotchi sat Hannah on his lap. "Lady Ferball's nephew demanded we pay him some newfangled tax when we sold our catch at Falmouth fish market. It was a robbery, Mr. Penhaligon. It left us nothing to feed our families on. When Mr. Bancroft explained to us that no one 'cept the king can make new taxes, we fishermen refused to pay. Lady Ferball's nephew was so angry, his whiskers turned purple. He said that no one would fish no more. The guard chained the boats together, then poured tar on the water to make sure we can't even fish for sprats in the harbor."

"And that's why Bancroft was arrested?" asked Penhaligon.

The hedgehog shook his head. "No. Mr. Bancroft is a very brave creature, Mr. Penhaligon. Much braver than me, I'm afraid." Hotchi lowered his head. "Sir Derek imposed a curfew. No creatures are allowed out of their homes past six bells. No lights are to be showing, and no one is allowed out of village."

"Bancroft broke the curfew?" asked Penhaligon, anxious to discover his brother's crime.

"Worse," explained Hotchi. "They put guards on the lane to the main road. Mr. Bancroft figured he could sneak by to fetch help. The village o' Sheepwash ain't that far away, once you're on the main road."

"Yes, I saw the sign," agreed Penhaligon.

Hotchi shortened his spines. "They caught 'im right away. He demanded to talk to Sir Derek—that's 'is name, Lady Ferball's nephew. He thought they'd come to some agreement." Hotchi reached for another pipe. "He didn't get a chance to speak. Sir Derek's guards, that spooky, sniffing crew that came with him, took 'im away. Said he'd be used as an example to the rest of us."

"Sir Derek sounds like a tyrant. Bancroft is a respectable member of the community, a school-teacher, no less. And as for those sniffy-nosed soldiers he has roaming around, it's enough to give the young ones nightmares." The look on the hoglets' faces told Penhaligon this was exactly what they had, night after night, when they weren't kept awake by their grumbling bellies.

"I don't think he's goin' to listen to anyone," said Hotchi. "We all be too weak to fight 'im now, all but starving, most of us. He's much too powerful, and he has the guards to protect 'im.

"Once, we tried net-fishing farther round the headland, but we was caught. As punishment, he burned our nets"—Hotchi lowered his voice—" 'cept the one I hid away real fast. He seems to know our every move. There's nothin' we can do. Escape while you can and send us help," the hedgehog urged.

"I'd like to, Hotchi," said Penhaligon. "But I'll not leave until I know Bancroft is safe. He's looked out for me all my life. If he's in trouble, then I must try to help him."

The hedgehog sighed. "Well then, you'd best sleep 'ere. There's nothin' to be done tonight." Hotchi pointed to a makeshift bed of straw in a corner.

Penhaligon didn't bother to ask for any food; he knew there wasn't any. He thought of the stew he'd imagined for dinner. Then he wished he hadn't, for it made his hunger pangs grow stronger. He remembered the bar of honey-apple in his pocket. It was sticky but edible. He peeled off the wrapper.

He was about to pop it into his mouth when he felt three pairs of eyes glued to him. "I'm not really hungry," he said, breaking the bar into three. "Would you young ones like this?"

Three pairs of grubby paws grabbed the honey-apple bar. The hoglets gobbled quickly, all except Hannah, who broke her piece again into three and offered some to her parents. Penhaligon wished he'd brought more, but how was he to know he would meet a family of starving hedgehogs?

He slept fitfully that night, dreaming of Bancroft in a dark dungeon, clapped in irons. The badger moaned Penhaligon's name and rattled his chains. Penhaligon awoke to the rattling of Mrs. Hotchi-witchi cleaning out the fire grate.

"Good morning, Mr. Penhaligon. I'm sorry we can't offer you no breakfast. Hotchi took the little 'uns to Rock Pool Beach, whelk hunting."

"Ah yes, I remember whelk hunting there with Bancroft last time I was here." Penhaligon smoothed his rumpled clothes. He would have given anything for a hot bath and a cup of rose-hip tea at that moment. "I'll go straight to the manor, I think, Mrs. Hotchi-witchi. The sooner Sir Derek sees sense, the better."

"Hotchi said it'd be best for you to stay 'ere and not be seen. Sir Derek 'as his spies, you know. You'd best talk to Hotchi first, my dear."

"Well, in that case, I'll go to Rock Pool Beach. If Hotchi believes Sir Derek to be that unreasonable, then perhaps I shall talk to his aunt, Lady Ferball, instead. She's a most gentle feline, as I recall. Bancroft introduced me last time I was here. In fact, we all had dinner together. I'm sure she doesn't realize what is going on, Mrs. Hotchi-witchi, or, I beg your pardon, is it Mrs. Witchi? It's such an unusual name."

"It's Hotchi-witchi. Heligan is my first name. Hotchi-witchi comes from a very old language not spoken in these parts anymore."

"I expect it has a fine meaning," said Penhaligon.

"Actually, it's the name of a stew."

Penhaligon disguised his surprise with a polite smile and bade good day to Mrs. Heligan Hotchi-witchi.

"Be careful, Mr. Penhaligon," she said. "The guard will take you, no questions asked."

# Trapped

## CHAPTER FIVE

O nce outside, Penhaligon made his way through the maze of alleyways by following the sound of the ocean. He found himself on the hilly street leading from the quay that he and Hotchi had hurried along the night before.

He continued up and away from the village, toward the headland. Penhaligon wondered if Sir Derek was the important news that Bancroft had mentioned in his letter. But then why did he not ask Penhaligon to bring help?

Nothing seemed to be making sense. The crown prince and half the king's army were just a few miles away in Falmouth, waiting for the arrival of Princess Katrina. Surely it couldn't be that hard to send a message to them?

The hill eventually flattened to a headland cliff that stretched like a finger into the sea. Here stood the red-

and-white-striped lighthouse that warned passing ships of the dangerous rocks at Rock Pool Beach.

Penhaligon spun around. He could see for miles across the flat countryside, a purple splash of the distant Moor, the closer green stripes of cauliflower fields. The view was breathtaking, and the breeze blew fresh through his fur. The village looked normal enough from here. There were no guard patrols, no tortured villagers. The day was so fine Penhaligon could almost believe everything that happened the night before was just a bad dream.

Porthleven was nestled in the center of the horseshoe-shaped bay. The cliffs rose gently on either side of the village, becoming steeper and craggier along the headlands that hugged the bay.

Across the bay, on the opposite headland from where he stood, was Brigand's Point. Penhaligon could see the grand Ferball Manor, surrounded by its sheltering wood of copper beech and chestnut trees. Farther along the headland, scrubby bushes, twisted into grotesque shapes by the constant winds, dotted the rocky outcrops.

A track forked off the manor road that turned into a narrow path, hewn into the cliff face. It was just a ledge in places, with a long drop to the rocky ocean if a creature's foot was misplaced.

Penhaligon had hiked the path with Bancroft, for eventually it rounded the headland, descending to a sheltered beach named Sandy Cove. Here Bancroft's house, a hull of a large boat upturned on the sand, was nestled in the dunes.

Penhaligon recalled the time he'd spent there, reading from the dozens of books Bancroft kept in his library, swimming in the ocean, and picnicking on cucumber sandwiches and lemonade.

The cliff path to Sandy Cove was a thrilling, wild hike, but in winter, when the chill winds blew off the sea, it was treacherous. So one summer, Penhaligon and Bancroft had built wooden steps from Sandy Cove up to Brigand's Point. Now it was an easy walk across the cliff top to Ferball Manor stables, where Bancroft taught the local youngsters.

A sharp cry of gulls interrupted Penhaligon's thoughts. He hastily continued past the lighthouse and toward Rock Pool Beach. The road became a path, spongy with pink sea thrift, and when he reached the tip of the headland, Penhaligon picked his way carefully down the cliff to the beach below.

The rocks were slick and dangerous, still damp from the sea that had now retreated, leaving a wealth of tide pools. Once safely at the bottom, he adjusted

his waistcoat and called to the distant figures he saw
stooping over the rock pools.

"Hey, Hotchi! Any luck?"

"Mr. Penhaligon, sir." He heard Hotchi's voice from
behind him.

"Where are you, Hotchi?"

"We be hiding in the rocks. Them over there are
Sir Derek's guards, and they now be coming your way.
Hurry back up the cliff. We'll meet you at 'ome."

The figures hurried toward him. Penhaligon realized these were not the creatures
he wanted to meet. He hastily

backed up the cliff path. But several more guards, sharp ferret faces peeking from under their helmets, had started down the path from the headland. He was trapped.

"Think! Think! Don't panic," he told himself. The tide was fully out. If he was fast enough, maybe he could reach Porthleven village along the beach. He jumped onto the sand and quickened his pace across the beach. He could smell the guards closing in behind him. His walk broke into a run.

The ferrets shouted at him, "Stop!" He wanted to look back to see how close they were but knew this would waste precious seconds. At least they haven't found Hotchi, thought Penhaligon.

This was actually his last thought before something hit him hard over the head and he sank into the deep sleep of the unconscious.

🪶 🪶 🪶 🪶

When he came to, Penhaligon found himself viewing an upside-down world. The burly ferret over whose shoulder he was slung growled at him to stop wiggling.

Penhaligon recognized the massive iron gates and

pink-flowered rhododendron bushes along the driveway of Ferball Manor. Trying to calm himself, he
counted the number of windows that glinted in the
morning sun, but he lost count before they reached
the grand house.

The guard set him down, and Penhaligon was
roughly ushered up the wide steps. One final prod
sent him flying over the threshold onto the hard marble floor.

"For goodness' sake, Captain Dredge, I've told you
before about throwing prisoners on the marble floor,"
howled a voice somewhere above Penhaligon's head.
"You must throw them through the tradesman's entrance
around back. I don't want the marble scratched."

"Sorry, your lordship," growled the burly ferret.

"I demand to see whoever's in charge here," said
Penhaligon, clambering up from his haunches and
brushing down his jacket.

"Not another one making demands," said the irritated
voice. "Sling him in the dungeon like that badger fellow. I'll question him after breakfast."

Penhaligon looked up at the sweeping red-carpeted
staircase. The voice belonged to a small, bony feline
wearing a purple silk dressing gown. His slicked-down,

black-and-tan-striped fur was parted severely across his head, while the tufts on his ears were waxed into curls, as were his whiskers. He regarded Penhaligon as though he were something nasty he'd stepped in.

"Just one minute—" said Penhaligon, shrugging off the ferret claws that held him. He was grabbed by Captain Dredge and bundled through a tapestry-curtained door before he could utter another syllable.

Down a steep, winding staircase they went, the chilled flagstones echoing their footsteps. Down and down the steps spiraled. Penhaligon knew they must be deep below Ferball Manor. It was cold, and he could smell the salty sea dampness. At least now he would see Bancroft, though he'd have preferred to meet over a pint of blackberry ale in the Cat and Fiddle instead of in a chilly dungeon.

The bottom of the steps opened into a room hewn from bare rock. Wooden kegs were stored against the wall, and shelves were lined with homemade jams, bottled fruits, and a large jar of pickled onions. A tiny slit of a window revealed an ocean view, and in the far corner there was a jagged hole chipped out of the floor large enough to fit a barrel of ale. Penhaligon heard waves crashing below, and sprays of water spit up through the floor. He shuddered, hoping he should never discover the purpose for such a hole.

Captain Dredge took a bulky ring of keys from a hook. He unlocked an iron-banded door that led off the storeroom. Penhaligon was pushed abruptly through it and locked in.

Light seeped in through another window slit. When his eyes became accustomed to the dim light, he saw a pile of rags in the corner, but the cell was otherwise empty.

"Where's the other prisoner?" shouted Penhaligon.

Captain Dredge laughed. "The badger? He went down this big hole out here yesterday."

"Yes, shame about that, wasn't it, Captain Dredge?" said the other guard. "Do you suppose he could swim?"

"Wouldn't much matter," said Dredge. "Those sharp rocks would soon turn him into badger meat." The ferrets hooted with laughter and headed back up the steps.

Penhaligon felt the room spin. There was a sick feeling in his stomach. He sank to the floor and wept for Bancroft.

## A Watery Fate

## CHAPTER SIX

It was some time later when the dungeon door flew open. Penhaligon, miserable, cold, and hungry, saw Captain Dredge standing in the doorway. His empty stomach twisted into a knot of anger.

"The boss wants to talk to you."

"Likewise," Penhaligon growled. He followed the ferret up the spiraled steps, across the marble hallway, and into a dining room.

At the end of a table that could have seated thirty foxes, Sir Derek was tearing into a barbecued chicken with extraordinarily long incisors. Penhaligon, like any other fox, couldn't stop his mouth from watering.

Sir Derek narrowed his eyes. "You are a stranger around these parts," he said, wiping his paws on a nearby ferret. The ferret squeaked as a claw caught his shoulder. A glare from Sir Derek was enough to silence him. "What were you doing on the beach? And where are my guards from the hill checkpoint?"

Penhaligon wanted to scream out, "Where is my brother?" He wanted to grab hold of this cruel, despicable creature and shake him until he admitted that Captain Dredge had lied, it wasn't Bancroft they'd pushed down the hole, it wasn't anybody, it was all a horrible nightmare, and in a moment he would wake up on the farmer's cart.

But he didn't wake up.

He would have to play the game until he could find a way out.

"I was collecting shells," said Penhaligon. "And I didn't see any guard on the hill." He didn't mention the monstrous figure that scared him half to death the night before.

"You expect me to believe that?" Sir Derek sneered. "A fox that collects shells, eh?

And a strange-looking fox at that. Never seen a fox with black-tipped fur. Are you foreign?" He picked his teeth with a long claw.

"I could ask you the same question," snapped Penhaligon. "I've never seen a cat with waxed ear fur before." One of the guards gave him a rough shove for his insolence.

"I don't expect a country fox with straw behind his rather large ears to appreciate the latest fashions. I think you're a spy, just like that badger fellow. I wouldn't be surprised if you even knew him. Do you?"

Even though a well-brought-up gentlefox would never lie, Penhaligon knew this situation called for desperate measures.

"I don't know who you're talking about. I don't associate with badgers."

"Don't lie to me, fox. You've been sent by the crown prince, haven't you?" Sir Derek stabbed his fork into the rest of the chicken. "Has he discovered my plans?"

Penhaligon sighed and picked the dungeon straw off his jacket. "As I said, I don't know what you're talking about. By the way, where is charming Lady Ferball? Her hospitality was quite gracious last I was here."

"You're a very nosy fox, aren't you? We have ways of dealing with nosy pests around here. Besides, you're spoiling my lunch." Sir Derek banged his clenched paw on the table. "Take him back to the dungeon."

"You'll never get away with this," Penhaligon shouted as he struggled to free himself from Captain Dredge's viselike grip.

Sir Derek laughed and sliced off a leg of chicken with one claw. "By the way, my aunt doesn't seem to be recovering, even though I see to her every whim myself."

Penhaligon's mind raced. This might be his last opportunity to save himself. "If I am a spy as you say, then surely 'they' will send others to see where I am."

"Stop!" yelled Sir Derek. Captain Dredge halted. "Yes, you are quite right." Sir Derek's brow furrowed. "I can't afford to have them find you at the manor. I'd better get rid of you now. Throw him down the sea hole."

"But, Sir Derek, the tide's not right," said Dredge.

"Don't bother me with specifics, Dredge. He'll either drown or be bashed to pieces on the rocks," said Sir Derek.

Penhaligon's hopes sank. So much for being smart.

He'd only speeded up his own execution. Captain Dredge dragged him from the room.

"You haven't heard the last of this," shouted Penhaligon.

"Yes, yes," said Sir Derek. "Tell it to the crabs."

Penhaligon stood at the edge of the dark gaping hole. The sea, in foamy turmoil below, promised a watery

grave. How he longed to be bored back in Ramble-on-the-Water.

"Any final requests?" Captain Dredge smiled as he asked.

"Just a question," said Penhaligon.

"What?" said Dredge.

"Do you always smell like rotting seagull carcass?" He never heard the answer, as Dredge, roaring in anger, pushed him into the hole.

He hit the water in an ungainly sprawl. Deeper and deeper he sank until Penhaligon thought his lungs would burst. He fought to the water's surface, but the weight of water in his tweed jacket pulled him farther down. White streams of bubbles rushed past his head.

"Don't panic. Don't panic," he told himself. He struggled with the jacket, but it stuck like a second skin. Frantic, he thrashed around, yanking at the sleeve. At last, he freed one arm, peeled the jacket from the other, and pushed his way to the surface. Finally, he gulped fresh air.

He was in a cavern, the rock having been carved by the waves of a thousand seasons. Daylight streamed through an opening that led to the ocean.

The sea came rushing in. Penhaligon felt himself rise. The powerful water pushed him toward the back of the cave, where jagged rocks encircled the cave like a shark's teeth. Another wave crashed in. This would be the one that rushed him to his fate. . . .

# Sir Derek's Plans Discovered

## CHAPTER SEVEN

Just as the wave lifted him up, there was a shout. "Grab this!"

A rope of braided sea kelp was thrown to him. Penhaligon lunged for this unexpected lifeline. He dug in his claws and prayed the kelp would not shred before he was pulled to safety. He grabbed his jacket just before it sank from view, flung it over the slimy rocks, and scrambled out before the wave could snatch him back.

Breathless, he looked up at his rescuer. "Bancroft!"

The badger's chubby gray face smiled. Wrapping his bulky arms around Penhaligon, he said, "Nice to see you, old chap."

"They told me you were dead."

"And so I would have been if it were not for the help of a special friend." From the shadows stepped a hunched and wretched figure with writhing, slimy

hair. Penhaligon gasped. It was the monster he'd seen on the road the night before. The creature whisked off the ragged seaweed hair and stood up straight.

"Lady Ferball?"

Lady Ferball's white-furred face broke into a grin. She straightened her flattened feline ears with a shake of her head. "I'm sorry I frightened you last night, Penhaligon. I was trying to escape Porthleven to get help. I thought you were one of my nephew's men. By the time I realized it was you, you'd run away." Her yellow eyes twinkled.

"Well, it is a very good disguise." Penhaligon shook the water from his fur, feeling a little foolish.

"I returned to tell Bancroft you were here," continued Lady Ferball. "We've been waiting for you."

Penhaligon gazed up at the hole in the roof, then at the churning sea. "I'm very glad you were, my friends."

A large wave soaked them as it crashed onto the rocks.

"Come on," said Bancroft. "The tide is coming in. We'd better get out of here before we all get swept away."

Penhaligon followed the others through a small tunnel leading away from the ocean and, Penhaligon realized, back underneath the manor.

Lady Ferball chatted merrily. "My nephew, Derek, thinks I'm locked up in my bedroom," she said, puffing up her thinning fur with frail paws. "He doesn't know about the secret passages. I overheard you talking to him earlier. That's how I knew you'd be down the sea hole anytime. I wear my disguise in case I'm seen. There's a delightful tale spreading amongst the guard about an ugly sea witch casting spells on all who are loyal to Derek. You should have heard the ferret guards on the hill shriek last night. I don't think Derek will be seeing them again."

"You aren't sick?" asked Penhaligon.

"Right as ninepence," replied Lady Ferball with a cat pounce to prove it.

The three sidled along the slippery tunnel. The cold walls were covered in dead seaweed and barnacles like little razors, sharp enough to cut if brushed up against.

"Bancroft," said Penhaligon, "I received your letter yesterday—why didn't you mention this trouble? Why didn't you ask for help? The king's Warthog Army marched right through Ramble-on-the-Water on their way to Falmouth. I could have brought them with me."

Bancroft's chuckle broke into a wheeze. "I believe you could have, Penhaligon. Trouble is when I wrote that letter, weeks ago, before the first day of the summer holidays, I might add, everything was fine. My mistake was to give the letter to Willie Wilkinson, one of my school boarders. Clearly his idea of 'mailing as soon as possible' is not the same as mine." Bancroft tried to hide a cough as he spoke. "And I thought he was one of my more reliable students."

"Are you unwell, Bancroft?" Penhaligon asked.

"Yes, he is," said Lady Ferball. "I wouldn't be surprised if he had pneumonia, being stuck in that old dungeon. The soaking he got yesterday was the last straw."

Penhaligon felt Bancroft's ears. "You're running a fever."

"I'll be fine. There are more important things we need to discuss."

They approached a lantern burning at the base of a rickety staircase. Lady Ferball put her paw to her mouth.

"Shhh! We have to be very quiet. We are inside the walls of the house." She pointed to the top of the stairs, and as they climbed, Penhaligon felt warmer. He hoped there was a secret passage to the kitchens; otherwise his growling stomach might give them all away.

Lady Ferball stopped. She pushed on a brick in the wall until a door slowly rolled open. Penhaligon found himself inside Lady Ferball's bedroom. It was decorated with powder-blue rugs and silk drapes and a carved headboard on the biggest bed he'd ever seen. A fire burned cheerily in the hearth.

He noticed a table by the sunlit window. It was laid with roasted meats, fruit, crusty bread, cheese, and green leafy stalks of celery sticking out from a glass vase.

Lady Ferball smiled. "Ah, I see Rowan has been busy."

"Rowan?" asked Penhaligon.

"My companion," she explained. She handed him a flowery robe and towel. "Hang your clothes by the fire. They'll be dry in no time."

Penhaligon was about to refuse the robe but decided his pride would not be hurt as much as his health if he didn't get his fur dry. He changed behind the dressing screen.

"Please help yourself to food, Mr. Penhaligon. You must be hungry. My nephew tries to starve me, but there's a secret passage to the kitchen too."

"I'd best see to Bancroft first," he said.

"Nonsense," said Bancroft. "You can't concentrate on an empty stomach. You'll probably mix me a cure for gout instead of a chill." Bancroft tried to laugh but ended up in a coughing fit.

Penhaligon sat him down and poured him a glass of blackcurrant juice.

"You eat, and I'll tell you why I really sent for you," said Bancroft.

"That must wait, my dear Bancroft. We must make plans straightaway," said Lady Ferball, slipping off her seaweed suit to soak it in a water bucket. "We are running out of time."

"Why can't you just send your nephew away?" asked Penhaligon, making himself a sandwich.

"Tried that," said Lady Ferball. "And threatened to report him to the king. That's when he locked me in my room. So I started to act as though my mind had gone. You know us old folk; we're always losing our marbles." She winked at Bancroft.

"There's a hedgehog in the village, Hotchi-witchi. He told me how Sir Derek stopped the fishermen from fishing because they wouldn't pay his taxes," said Penhaligon. He savored a large bite of sandwich.

"That's true," Bancroft wheezed. "But now Sir Derek doesn't need their tax money. He has a new and more dastardly plan." The badger signaled to Lady Ferball, who pulled out a map from behind her dresser. He lowered his voice. "Did you notice how dark the village was last night?"

Penhaligon nodded. "Even the lighthouse lamp was out."

"Sir Derek doesn't want ships to see the Porthleven lighthouse, or any light in Porthleven, come to that. Except for the one he's going to light." Bancroft's eyes narrowed. "Lady Ferball overheard his plans. Sir Derek intends to wreck the ships from Spatavia. On board is Princess Katrina—"

"And her substantial dowry," interrupted Penhaligon, remembering the discussion in the Warren Arms the previous day.

"Like wreckers in the old days," said Bancroft. "He'll light a beacon somewhere along the cliffs." He pointed to the map. "Problem is finding out where. The ships will think it's the Rock Pool Beach lighthouse, warning them of the rocks."

"And if the ships aren't in the place where they think they are—" chimed in Lady Ferball.

"They'll be too close to shore and"—Bancroft made a slicing gesture across his neck—"that will be that."

"But dozens of lives could be lost," said Penhaligon.

"I don't think he much cares about that," said Lady Ferball. "Bancroft and I intend to stop him if we can. But there isn't much time. The ships will be in sight of Porthleven tonight." Lady Ferball let out a long

breath. "I'm afraid I feel somewhat responsible for this whole mess."

"How could you be?" asked Penhaligon.

Lady Ferball gestured around her. "I have this large house, and an even larger fortune, and no offspring. Normally, everything would pass to Sir Derek. But

Derek has always been a lazy, vain, greedy, unscrupulous little . . . well, let's just say he's the runt of the litter." The old cat lowered her voice to a whisper. "Some say there's much Highland wildcat on his father's side of the family. So, I decided I would spend my fortune now to improve my beautiful Porthleven." Lady Ferball patted Bancroft on the back. "Poor Bancroft. Ever since he answered my request for a schoolmaster, I've been promising a new schoolhouse."

"The stables work well enough, Lady Ferball. Just a little drafty." Bancroft smiled.

"Then there's the hospital we'd build. There isn't a hospital for miles around these parts. Oh, and a library," said Lady Ferball. "Even a new boathouse.

"Only trouble was Derek heard about it, through my sister, of course. She always was a blabbermouth. He arrived, along with that motley crew of ferrets he calls his guard, to convince me I was making a mistake. He was very angry when I wouldn't change my mind. So his next scheme was to take charge. I was too sick to protest at the time. He tried to impose the fishing tax, which, as you know, didn't work. When he heard about the Spatavian ships, he decided to grab his fortune the old-fashioned way."

"We don't have much of a chance against his whole

army," said Penhaligon. "Someone must escape Porthleven and warn the crown prince. Falmouth isn't too far." Penhaligon paced back and forth.

"That was my plan last night, and if I'd succeeded, the crown prince and his army might be here now," said Lady Ferball. "Penhaligon, we're on our own and out of time. Will you help us?"

Ramble-on-the-Water had never seemed so far away as it did to Penhaligon at that moment. "Of course I will, my lady," he said. "Do you have a plan, Bancroft?"

Bancroft mopped his brow. "I think maybe I should lie down for a moment."

## Friend or Foe?

## CHAPTER EIGHT

A nasty wheeze sounded from deep within the badger's chest. His fever was worse. "Bancroft, my friend, you really aren't well," said Penhaligon. "You should be in bed."

"Don't be fussing. I'm all right. Just a bit of a chill."

Lady Ferball frowned. "I should have had that nasty dungeon sealed up years ago, but it is the perfect temperature for storing my ginger ale and pickled onions." She sighed, mumbling, "I wonder if I'll ever be making ginger ale again. Derek's ferrets have drunk nearly all of my stock and eaten all but one jar of onions."

"I must make a remedy for your chest, Bancroft. I'll need some lungwort, swallowwort, elder flower, and chestnut leaves," said Penhaligon.

"We have everything in the garden except swallowwort," said Lady Ferball. "But I expect Rowan will know where a patch of it grows."

Bancroft protested but was too weak to put up much of a fight when Penhaligon put him to bed. They dressed him in one of Lady Ferball's lace night-caps and her bed jacket. Anyone who happened to enter the room would assume it was the old cat in bed. He yawned. "I am quite tired," he finally admitted. "I'll have just a little nap."

"That's right, Bancroft, a little nap," said Penhaligon. "I wish Sir Derek and his ferrets would have a little nap too."

"I remember when you made all the school bullies fall asleep," Bancroft chuckled sleepily.

"I'm sure Lady Ferball doesn't want to hear about school-day pranks," said Penhaligon quickly.

"On the contrary, my dear boy, it sounds fascinating," she said.

The badger continued. "Penhaligon made barley-sugar candies containing a powerful sleeping potion. The bullies stole his candy, as usual, and they all fell asleep during a math test. They received detention and extra math homework for a whole week." Bancroft's smile faded as he drifted off.

"Penhaligon! I'm surprised at you," Lady Ferball chastised.

Penhaligon shrugged. "It was easy. They were

always taking my candy. They gave the potion to themselves." Penhaligon also remembered the trouble he'd been in when Menhenin had found out.

"My ginger ale!" announced Lady Ferball. "The guards are always taking that too."

Penhaligon stroked his ears thoughtfully. "Hmm. It's so simple. But it might work. If we can put most of the guard to sleep, it may give us a chance to relight the lighthouse lamp, and the ships will be able to sail by safely." Penhaligon shook his head. "What am I saying? How could we possibly make sure that all the guards drank the ginger ale? There must be dozens of them."

"Well, ferrets are bullies, and bullies love to steal candy from children. . . ." Lady Ferball smiled mischievously. "We could enlist some little helpers."

"But it will take too long to collect herbs, prepare Bancroft's cure and a sleeping potion, make sugar candy, and then distribute the candy to the village children, let alone put the sleeping potion in the ginger ale." Penhaligon sank into a chair, defeated.

"It's time you met my companion, Rowan. She'll help you, don't you worry."

"She's trustworthy?" asked Penhaligon.

"But of course. She came to me as a young orphan.

They found her near the Moor almost frozen to death. She's like my own flesh and blood."

Lady Ferball pulled on a long tasseled rope. Almost immediately they heard light footsteps in the hallway. There was a brief knock before the bedroom door was unlocked.

"Rowan," said Lady Ferball. "I want you to meet someone."

Penhaligon studied the young fox carefully. Her soft vixen fur was a deep ruddy brown, the color of rowan-tree berries. There was a delicate tilt to her head as she walked across the room. She stared back, suspicion in her amber eyes.

"Who are you?" she demanded.

Penhaligon shifted uncomfortably. He felt at a disadvantage standing there wearing Lady Ferball's flowery robe instead of his usual tweeds.

"Now, Rowan, it's all right. This is Mr. Penhaligon Brush, a friend of Bancroft's," said Lady Ferball. "He has a plan that will save Porthleven and the Spatavian ships."

Rowan raised her eyebrows, unconvinced. "How clever of him. And will that be before or after he changes out of your flowered silk robe?"

Penhaligon's ears twitched. Lady Ferball appeared not to notice the vixen's sharp tongue.

"Rowan, first we need to gather herbs for Bancroft's medicine and a sleeping potion. Make up some story to tell the guards—cut some roses for my room or something," said Lady Ferball.

"Poor Mr. Bancroft," said Rowan. "I should have insisted he take my mixture earlier."

Penhaligon cooled the badger's forehead with a damp cloth. Bancroft moaned, slightly delirious.

"We need lungwort, swallowwort, elder flower, and chestnut leaves, if you please, Miss Rowan," said Penhaligon in the most commanding voice he could muster while wearing a flowery robe.

"I am aware of what herbs are needed, Mr. Penhaligon," said Rowan stiffly. She pushed past Penhaligon to adjust Bancroft's pillows. "We will have to substitute maidenhair fern for swallowwort for now." She listened to Bancroft's chest. Penhaligon frowned and picked up Bancroft's paw to check his pulse.

"I disagree. If we give him maidenhair now, we won't be able to give him the swallowwort later. The two are incompatible."

"I realize they're incompatible; I'm not a nincompoop," said Rowan. "I just feel he needs the fern to loosen his breathing."

Penhaligon was about to answer when . . .

"How wonderful to have two expert herbalists around," chirped Lady Ferball. "Rowan is marvelous with herbal cures, Penhaligon. I'm sure she saved my life when I was so ill."

The two foxes glared at each other.

"Anyway," hissed Rowan. "The only patch of swallowwort is a ways from here."

"How far?" asked Penhaligon, checking Bancroft's ears.

"Rock Pool Beach, on the cliffs next to the light-house. Sir Derek has guards there," said Rowan, feeling Bancroft's snout.

Bancroft moaned in a sleepy voice, "Will you both stop fussing like nervous ninnies? I'm not that sick." Bancroft coughed again.

"I didn't see any guards when I was there earlier, just on the beach. His ears are almost on fire with fever," said Penhaligon. "We have to give him something and quickly."

"Exactly. I'll gather what I can from my herb garden. We don't have time for a trip to Rock Pool Beach," said Rowan.

"We will also need some valerian, catmint, and sweet woodruff," said Penhaligon, then muttered under his

breath, "unless you have any bright ideas on sleeping potions too."

"Actually," said Rowan, whose hearing was very sharp, "there's a hops bush in the kitchen garden. But I hardly think Bancroft needs a sleeping potion."

Lady Ferball quickly explained the plan to drug as many guards as possible.

"Sounds ridiculous to me," said Rowan.

Penhaligon rolled his eyes.

"Still, I suppose it's the only plan we have so far. I'd better go and steal some sugar. What flavor are you making, blackcurrant?"

"Barley."

"Hmm. Typical." Rowan's skirts swished briskly as she left the room.

"So what do you think of my Rowan?" asked Lady Ferball.

"She's very . . . efficient," said Penhaligon, wondering what was wrong with barley sugar.

"I get tired just watching her," said Lady Ferball. "You'll have to forgive her sharp tongue. She's very protective of me. She was raised by Romany wolves, you know. That's where she learned her healing skills. They are the best healers of all."

"Romany wolves?" Penhaligon couldn't believe his ears. "But the Romany wolves are—I mean, no one's seen one in years, have they? I thought they were just about extinct . . . aren't they?"

"Probably almost are, now," said Lady Ferball sadly. "The old female wolf that adopted Rowan—Mennah, I think her name was—died the winter I found Rowan." Lady Ferball sniffed.

"All the stories I ever heard about Romany wolves told of savage creatures who'd steal young ones and kill any poor soul who wandered onto the Moor," said Penhaligon.

"Bah! Do you always believe everything you hear, young fox?" Lady Ferball studied his face.

Penhaligon couldn't think what to say, so he didn't say anything. Instead he studied Bancroft's map, tracing the coastline with his paw, trying to visualize where Sir Derek could wreck the ships.

His mind kept jumping back to Rowan. How could Lady Ferball trust someone who'd lived as a Romany wolf for so long? He should keep an eye on her for all their sakes.

But now he needed to concentrate. There were so many dangerous outcrops of rocks shown on the map, even apart from Rock Pool Beach. Any one of them would provide a watery grave for the Spatavians.

Penhaligon watched his friend toss fitfully in the huge bed. He told Lady Ferball, "I need to find Hotchi-witchi. He may know where the ferrets have been building a beacon. If we can sabotage it, or even set it alight before nightfall, then even if we fail to relight the lighthouse, the ships will stay far out to sea rather than risk sailing too close to shore."

"Good idea, Penhaligon. Rowan will help you find Hotchi. She knows the lay of the land, where the guard posts are and suchlike."

Penhaligon started to protest, but Lady Ferball held up her paw. "Now, Penhaligon, I know you're a gentle-fox and are worried about Rowan's safety, but believe me, Rowan is quite capable of handling herself." Penhaligon didn't doubt that for a moment.

When Rowan returned, she removed the roses from her basket to reveal the herbs, onions, and other paraphernalia they would need to make the potions. She ground the herbs for Bancroft's medicine in a stone mortar almost identical to the one Penhaligon used in the shop.

"Where did you find a mortar such as this?" he asked.

"It belonged to my mother," she answered, intently grinding with the heavy pestle.

Penhaligon watched carefully, but she made no mistakes. He fed the sweet oil into Bancroft's mouth. Rowan placed a hot poultice of onion skins and mustard leaves on his wheezing chest. She seems civilized, thought Penhaligon as he watched her spread the mix. But for all her fair gentleness, she made him feel uneasy. He would keep his wits about him.

They set to work on the sleeping potion. The foxes chopped and pummeled, measured and mixed, keeping a watchful eye on each other's work.

Lady Ferball stirred a pan of sugar until it melted to a thick golden goo. A little lemon, a lot of sleeping potion, and it was done. They pulled the goo into long strands and chopped the strands into little pieces before the sugar cooled into hard amber chunks.

"I have an idea how to get the candy to some youngsters, but who will put sleeping potion into the ginger ale?" asked Rowan.

"I'll do it," said Penhaligon. "I'll climb up the hole in the dungeon floor and pour it into the kegs."

"You are a fit young fox, Penhaligon," said Lady Ferball, "but that would be too dangerous a climb."

"And how do you get back?" asked Rowan. "Jump in the sea again? No, I'll go. I'll just tell Captain Dredge that Lady Ferball would like some of her own ginger ale."

"And what if he says no?" said Penhaligon.

"Penhaligon's right, Rowan," said Lady Ferball. "He probably would say no just to spite me. Besides, Penhaligon needs your help finding Hotchi. *I* shall go to the dungeon in my seaweed costume. If there are any guards around, I'll scare the britches off them."

"It's too dangerous," said Rowan.

"Nonsense. You know I'm right," said Lady Ferball.

"And we'd better hurry. It'll be suppertime before you know it. They'll be changing the guard and fetching another keg of ginger ale. I don't know how many of the vermin we can knock off to sleep, but if we don't hurry, we'll miss our chance at any of 'em."

## On the Run

## CHAPTER NINE

Everything was ready. The barley-sugar drops gleamed like amber, and a glass bottle of sleeping potion was ready for action. Penhaligon had to admit that he would not have been able to prepare everything without the vixen's help.

Just then, footsteps echoed in the hallway. They stopped outside the bedroom door. A fist pounded on the wood.

"Who is it?" Rowan asked.

"Sir Derek. I demand you open the door. I wish to see my aunt immediately."

Lady Ferball grabbed hold of a surprised Penhaligon and pulled him under the bed.

"Er . . . Lady Ferball is sleeping, Sir Derek. She is still most unwell."

"Open the door before I have it broken down," he roared.

Seeing the two safely hidden and Bancroft tucked in tight, Rowan unlocked the door. Sir Derek pushed past her, his narrow eyes searching the room as keenly as one of his ferret-faced guards.

Rowan gasped, realizing that all the evidence from their potion making as well as the telltale food and glasses were still on the table. She sat on the table edge and spread her skirts to hide the mess.

"I trust you with a key to this door for my convenience, not yours. You'll open up more promptly in the future."

"Yes, Sir Derek." Rowan bowed her head.

"What's that smell?" His nose twitched.

"Smell?" echoed Rowan.

"Smells like seaweed. And something else. . . ." Sir Derek walked up to the sleeping "Lady Ferball," who was snoring loudly. "Badgers!"

"Badgers?" Rowan almost squeaked.

"Will you stop echoing me?" roared Sir Derek.

"Sorry, Sir Derek. It's probably her ladyship's mustard poultice," said Rowan.

"Does she always make such a noise?" he asked crossly, poking at the mustard poultice and wincing.

"Lady Ferball" launched into a series of loud snorts.

"I think it's because she is so ill, sir," said Rowan.

"You are following my orders and keeping the door locked at all times?"

"Yes, of course, Sir Derek," said Rowan.

From under the bed, Penhaligon and Lady Ferball could see the small, fluffy pom-poms on the toes of Sir Derek's slippers. Lady Ferball started to giggle.

"What was that?" asked Sir Derek.

"I'm sorry, sir. I'm hungry. I always giggle when I'm hungry," said Rowan.

"I don't like giggling. Giggling is most offensive. I suggest you *find* yourself something to eat before you *find* yourself in the dungeon."

Rowan lowered her eyes. "Yes, Sir Derek," she said.

Sir Derek walked to the door. "A few things are going to change around here after tonight. I don't think you'll have much to laugh at then. Call me as soon as my aunt wakes up." He walked out, slamming the door behind him.

Penhaligon scrambled from under the bed, then helped Lady Ferball, who was laughing uncontrollably by now.

"I've never noticed those slippers before. Aren't they a hoot?"

"Lady Ferball, please be serious," said Penhaligon. "We have no time to lose."

"Of course," Lady Ferball agreed, trying not to smile. The fox took just a minute to change back into his stiff, salty, but at least now dry clothes. He was certain his appearance was quite different from that of the well-dressed fox who left Ramble-on-the-Water.

He checked his patient. Bancroft was breathing a little easier now, although his fever was still high. Penhaligon realized he still hadn't discovered what Bancroft's important news was, but nothing could be as important as saving the Spatavian ships and seeing his friend recover.

At last they were ready to leave. Penhaligon grabbed a napkin and filled it with bread and a wedge of cheese from the table.

"How can you think of your stomach at a time like this?" muttered Rowan. She hugged Lady Ferball, who'd changed back into her slithery seaweed costume. "Please be careful, Lady."

"Don't you worry about me." Lady Ferball scooped the barley-sugar drops into a pink silk scarf and gave them to Rowan. "Here, don't forget these!"

Penhaligon stuffed some apples into his jacket pockets. "Good-bye, Lady Ferball. Good luck."

"And to you, young fox." She rolled open the secret door, and the two foxes slipped into the darkened passage.

Penhaligon stuck close behind as Rowan guided the way through the maze of corridors. He tried to take note of the rights and lefts, ups and downs, but small spaces made him nervous, and all he could think about was finding some fresh air. All at once they were climbing up through a trapdoor in the garden greenhouse.

Penhaligon gulped the fresh air, thankful to be back in the daylight. They were close to the kitchen entrance of the manor house. Ferret armor was stacked against the wall, along with spears and shields.

"What is all the armor doing there?" asked Penhaligon.

"The ferrets remove it before they go inside," said Rowan. "Sir Derek's orders. He doesn't like the furniture scratched.

"Now pay attention. This is the tricky part," she said. "See, up there on the roof? There are two guards. If they spot us, they'll raise the alarm, and we're done for."

They left the cover of the greenhouse and crept through the bushes. "Now we have to cross the lawn to those trees over there, and we'll be safe." Rowan inched ahead.

"Wouldn't it be better to go around the lawn so we can't be seen?" asked Penhaligon.

"They'd hear us or smell us for sure. We can cross the lawn in a matter of seconds, too fast for them to pick up a scent. Just wait until they have their backs to us."

Before he had time to argue, Rowan hissed, "Now!"

She sprinted across the grass. Penhaligon quickly caught up and overtook her. He reached the cover of trees on the other side.

Just then, Rowan's foot caught in her skirts. She

tripped. With a little cry, she landed hard. "Drat these idiotic skirts!" she cursed.

The guards looked down. "Hey! You! What do you think you're doing?" one of them shouted.

Penhaligon hadn't noticed Rowan's fall. He looked back when the guard shouted.

"Carry on! Make a run for it," Rowan gasped.

Penhaligon hesitated. "Flaming foxgloves," he muttered. He ran back to help Rowan. He scooped her off the lawn. He staggered a bit. She weighed more than he had thought. "What did you eat for lunch?"

"I can manage," said Rowan, scowling. She wriggled onto her hind legs. The two foxes ran for their lives amid the angry shouts of the guard. They ducked into the trees and kept running. Finally, Rowan stopped and sank to the ground to nurse her twisted ankle.

"Phew! That was close," said Penhaligon. "At least we're safe now."

Rowan brushed the grass off her skirts and scowled. "No, we're not. I could easily have made up some story as to why I was in the garden, but oh no, you have to play the hero and rescue me. Now Sir Derek knows that you're still alive and that you and I and probably Lady Ferball are in cahoots. The guards will be extra vigilant. Lady Ferball is at great risk, and I am an outlaw."

"I—I'm sorry," stammered Penhaligon. "I didn't mean to . . ."

There was no point in trying to explain. She was right. He'd acted without thinking. An icy chill made Penhaligon's fur prickle. If Sir Derek discovered the sea witch to be Lady Ferball, then he'd surely also discover that it was Bancroft who lay snoring in her bed.

## Pickled Fox

## CHAPTER TEN

"I t's too late to turn around," said Rowan when Penhaligon suggested they return to warn Lady Ferball and Bancroft. "We'd be caught for sure. Then we'd all end up down the sea hole."

She hoisted the back hem of her skirts through her legs and tucked it into her waistband. "I need some britches," she announced.

Penhaligon turned his head.

"What's the matter?" She glared. "Never seen a vixen in britches before?"

Penhaligon pretended to check his pocket watch, which he discovered had stopped. "We'd better be getting on," he said.

"First, we're going to need some help," said Rowan. She stretched her slender neck to the sky and closed her eyes. A low howl wound its way up her throat and out into the treetops.

Penhaligon shivered. It was not like anything he'd heard before, yet it stirred something familiar deep inside him. Rowan lowered her head and gave Penhaligon a scornful glance. Moments later the nearby undergrowth rustled. Someone or something was coming their way.

"We should hide," said Penhaligon. "Quick."

Rowan tossed her head and laughed. "No need," she said. At that moment two small, furry figures emerged from the bushes.

Penhaligon's snout dropped open. There in front of him stood two ragged, shaggy creatures. "Wolf cubs," he managed to blurt out.

"Let me introduce my friends," said Rowan, who was obviously enjoying Penhaligon's discomfort immensely. "This is Dora." She put her arm around the smaller of the two. "And this is Donald." She ruffled the dark, spiky fur on the wolf cub's head. The two cubs grinned, displaying their fine, long teeth.

"How do you do," said Penhaligon to the wolf urchins. "Excuse us, would you?"

He took Rowan to one side. "Have you quite lost your senses? These youngsters are wolves. They're not to be trusted."

"Excuse me," said Rowan in a voice that was too

loud. "I'd trust them with my life. I've known them since they were born; in fact, I helped bring them into the world. You, on the other paw, I just met, and so far we've nearly been caught and you've brought danger to a person I love dearly, Lady Ferball."

"That was hardly my fault," Penhaligon began to protest.

"Who better to hand out the candy to the local youngsters and explain why not to eat it but to let the ferrets steal it? And," she continued before Penhaligon could respond, "Hotchi lives on the other side of the quay. We're going to need a diversion to get past the quayside guard posts." She gestured to the cubs. "They are it."

The cubs bowed as if on cue, ready for as much mischief as they could cause. Penhaligon sighed. Nothing good would come of this, he was sure.

Rowan explained their plan to the cubs as they followed alongside the Porthleven road. They kept themselves hidden in the undergrowth and headed toward the village. Dora suddenly halted and tugged frantically at Rowan's sleeve, using paw gestures that Penhaligon took as a kind of sign language.

"Quick! Hide," said Rowan. "Dora says the ferrets are approaching."

Penhaligon was just about to say he didn't hear Dora say anything when Rowan yanked him into the bushes. A cloud of dust moved along the road. Penhaligon heard the clanking of armor as a small band of ferrets came running toward them.

They halted only a few feet away from the creatures hidden in the bushes. Penhaligon hardly dared breathe. Surely they must have been spotted? He recognized the gravelly voice of Captain Dredge.

"Right, you lot," Dredge barked at his ferrets. "Get down to the guard posts in the village and tell them to be on the lookout for Lady Ferball's companion-maid and a snotty-looking fox in a tweed jacket."

Penhaligon flushed with indignation. He thought he heard Rowan snigger.

"Sir Derek promised a financial reward for whoever catches them," Dredge quietly added to himself, "though I wouldn't hold your breath." He sniffed the air as though he smelled something suspicious.

"What is it, sir?" asked one of the guards.

"It's hard to tell, seeing you lot haven't had a bath in I don't know how long," said Dredge. The ferrets made a strange hacking sound that Penhaligon supposed was laughter. Dredge continued, "We'll catch 'em soon enough. There's nowhere for them to run.

Alert the guards and then report back to me at the manor. Sir Derek needs my special help questioning Lady Ferball." The ferrets started hacking again. "Now get to it," ordered Dredge.

The soldiers ran toward the village while Dredge sniffed the air one more time before jogging back toward the manor.

"They're bound to find Bancroft," said Penhaligon when it was safe to talk. "What are we to do?"

"I'm as worried as you," said Rowan. "But we'd never reach the manor before Dredge. Besides, Sir Derek may have already discovered Bancroft. If we're caught too, then we're all doomed, including the Spatavian ships."

Penhaligon sighed. Rowan was right. He looked at his small band of saboteurs and sighed. "Come on, then. What are we waiting for?"

🐾 🐾 🐾 🐾

Sir Derek paced back and forth across the manor house roof while the two ferret guards cowered in the corner.

"What do you mean, they just suddenly appeared out of nowhere? How can anyone appear from no-where? Either you two were asleep or—"

"No, no, no, honestly, your lordship. We wasn't asleep, was we, Bert?"

Bert nodded his head as though it were on a spring. Then, as he saw Sir Derek's eyes narrow, he realized he was making the wrong response. His nods turned to side-to-side shakes with a couple of nods at the end just in case he still hadn't got it right.

"Get down there and search the grounds. You can bet there's an entrance to a secret passage. Whoever finds it will receive a financial reward."

"Yes, sir!" said Bert and Alfred. They bundled through the rooftop door, tripping each other in the process.

"Fools!" muttered Sir Derek. He descended the stairs two at a time until he reached the corridor where Lady Ferball's chambers were located. He knocked on the door. There was no reply. He tried the door handle. It was locked. He felt around his belt for his chain of keys, then realized he'd given them to the cook to open the food cupboard.

"Drat," he murmured. "One has to keep everything locked up with those ferrets around." He strode down the corridor to the great staircase.

Captain Dredge was entering the front door.

"Dredge!" he roared. "Where are the spare keys?"

"In the cellar storeroom, sir."

"Well, don't just stand there, go and get them."

Dredge headed toward the tapestry-curtained door.

"No, wait. I'll go myself. I want to check the kegs of ginger ale, anyway. I bet you thieving ferrets have nearly drunk us dry." Sir Derek laughed when he saw Dredge's eyes narrow. "Just a joke, Dredge. By the way, tell your troops they'd better eat well at supper. This will be their last decent meal until we reach the New Land. And personally, I can't wait to be out of this wretched drafty dump."

🕯 🕯 🕯 🕯

Penhaligon, Rowan, and the cubs hid behind the stone wall of the Cat and Fiddle. The fishing boats bobbed up and down in the tar-slicked water. There were a few villagers around and plenty of ferret-faced guards. It was impossible to cross the open quayside without being seen.

"This could be harder than we thought," said Rowan.

"Look! There's Hotchi-witchi," said Penhaligon. Sure enough, the spiny hedgehog was cleaning his fish barrels on the quayside. Hannah played beside him with her ball.

"Hotchi!" Penhaligon called as loud as he dared. It was no good; he was too far away. *"Hot-chi-wit-chi,"* again he tried, without luck.

"Shhh!" hissed Rowan. "You'll get us all caught."

"Listen. I have a plan. If your friends distract the guards," Penhaligon told her, "we may be able to hitch a ride in Hotchi's barrel." Rowan nodded and whispered instructions to the cubs, giving them the scarf filled with the barley-sugar drops.

Hannah looked up as the two wolf cubs approached her. She recognized them at once and waved. The cubs used their paw signs again, and Hannah seemed to understand perfectly. Squinting her eyes in his direction, she saw Penhaligon and smiled. Penhaligon was worried she might accidentally give them away, but he needn't have. Hannah whispered in her father's ear; he signaled Penhaligon to wait.

The youngsters started to play. Hannah threw her ball to Donald. Donald threw it to Dora, who bounced the ball back to Hannah. The ferret-faced guard standing nearest ignored them.

"Hannah knows the cubs?" asked Penhaligon.

"Of course," said Rowan. "They go to school together."

"Does Bancroft know that they're, well, you know . . . wolves?"

Rowan rolled her eyes. "I imagine he's noticed."

Hannah bounced the ball hard. It hit the ferret guard. He smiled at her and handed her the ball. She stuck out her tongue.

"Why you spiny little . . ." He reached for her, but Dora pushed him hard. He fell backward over Donald, perched on all fours behind him.

The three youngsters darted away in different directions. The villagers pointed and laughed at the ferret guard sprawled on the ground. Other guards came to help him.

"After them, after them," he cried.

Amid the confusion, Hotchi, unnoticed, hurried over to the waiting foxes.

"Mr. Penhaligon," he said. "We'd given you up after you was caught."

"I almost gave up on myself, Hotchi," said Penhaligon. "Will the youngsters be all right? They won't get caught, will they?"

Hotchi laughed. "They never have yet. Those alleyways are a maze unless you know your way around."

"We must talk, Hotchi," said Rowan. "Many lives could be lost tonight. We need your help."

"Don't you think I got everyone in enough trouble, Miss Rowan?" said Hotchi unhappily.

"Hotchi, it wasn't your fault. You had no other choice," said Rowan.

"It's not safe to talk here," said the hedgehog.

"I have an idea to get us past the guard post, Hotchi." Penhaligon told him of his plan.

Hotchi hurried back to his barrel and heaved it onto his handcart. He wheeled the cart behind the fence. "Jump in," he said. "Sorry about the smell. I usually keep my pickled herrings in here."

Rowan and Penhaligon squeezed into the barrel. "Flaming foxgloves!" was all Penhaligon managed to say before Hotchi slapped on the lid and trundled away with the two fugitives.

Everything went according to plan until they reached the guard post. "Halt!" commanded the guards.

"What yer got in the barrel, Spiny?" one of the ferrets asked.

"Nothing?" said Hotchi, not sounding at all sure.

"Well, let's take a look at nothing, shall we?" said the guard.

"Wait, I got a better idea," said another ferret. The poor hedgehog trembled. "Sure you aren't hiding any runaway foxes in there?" he asked.

"N-n-no, sir," stammered Hotchi.

"Good. Then you won't mind if I check. My way." He drew his sword.

Inside the smelly barrel, Penhaligon heard the draw

of steel from its sheath. His breath caught in a gasp. Rowan covered his snout with her paw.

"B-b-b-b-but, sir." Hotchi's stutter was even worse. "It's so s-s-stinky. Old f-f-fish, you know."

"Don't worry, I don't intend to take off the lid. That would be too much trouble."

Penhaligon had an awful feeling in the pit of his stomach. Now it was Rowan's turn to gasp. Penhaligon felt for her paw and held it tight.

The guard rammed his sword through the barrel until the shining point showed out of the other side.

Hotchi's jaw fell open.

## Sabotage

## CHAPTER ELEVEN

"Didn't hear any screams," said the ferret. "So you can go."

Hotchi pushed the handcart as fast as he could to his cottage. "Oh my goodness. Oh my goodness. Oh my goodness," he repeated over and over until he reached home.

Inside the cottage, he feverishly worked off the lid. "Oh, Heli, come quick, sommat awful has just 'appened." Hotchi peered into the barrel, expecting the worst.

"Ouch!" complained Rowan as Penhaligon clambered out, accidentally stepping on her sore ankle.

He rubbed the side of his head. "You had your elbow in my ear the whole way." Penhaligon brushed down his clothes. "I think I'll have to throw this jacket away."

There was a large rip through the pocket where the ferret's sword had sliced it, miraculously missing any part of him or Rowan. The apple in Penhaligon's pocket was cut in two. Rowan rolled her eyes. Feeling faint, Hotchi keeled over in a chair.

Mrs. Hotchi-witchi saw to her husband while the Hotchi hoglets danced around. "Mr. Penhaligon, Mr. Penhaligon. Mr. Penhaligon has come to save us."

Rowan raised an eyebrow. "Popular around here, aren't you?" she asked.

Penhaligon ignored her, turning instead to Hannah. "I'm glad to see you escaped the guard, young lady," he told her. "Where are your partners in crime?"

"They'll be back soon," said Hannah, giving the fox a hug.

Penhaligon pulled out the bread and cheese from his pocket. Then, like a magician, he produced the rest of the apples.

"This one is already cut up for you," he said, holding the sword-sliced halves. The youngsters squealed with delight.

"You never said you were taking food for starving hedgehogs," Rowan said rather sheepishly.

"You never asked," he replied.

Later, the little hoglets, bellies content, curled into spiny balls and slept, except for Hannah, who listened quietly while the grown-ups talked.

"But someone must have seen something. How

could a huge beacon be built without being noticed?" asked Penhaligon as patiently as he could. He was tired and upset. He desperately wanted to be home next to his fire in his comfortable chair.

Hotchi shrugged. "No one's allowed out the village, see." He scratched his chin. "There's one might know. Old Amon of the clock tower. He takes care of the harbor clock. There's a grand view from the tower. He used to work in the lighthouse when he was younger."

"Then we should find him," said Rowan.

"It would be safer for me to fetch him," said Mrs. Hotchi-witchi. "But it may take some time. He's not as spry as he used to be."

"Be careful, Heli," said Hotchi, kissing her cheek.

"I'll be back soon as I can," she promised.

♙ ♙ ♙ ♙

The "sea witch" crept through the secret passageway, clutching the sleeping potion Penhaligon had made. Pushing a stone lever in the wall, she slid through the gap that opened before her. Looking left and right, Lady Ferball hurried toward the dungeon. There were no guards, and a set of keys hung on a hook outside the dungeon door.

"Rats," she cursed. "Nobody for me to scare."

She removed the cork stoppers from the kegs of ginger ale and poured in the sleeping potion. "That will teach them to drink all my best ginger ale." For good measure she poured some into the one remaining jar of pickled onions.

Lady Ferball was about to drop the empty bottle down the sea hole when someone grabbed her shoulder.

♟ ♟ ♟ ♟

Penhaligon sighed. "There aren't enough of us," he said, pacing the wooden floor of Hotchi's cottage. "We need to find and destroy Sir Derek's beacon, light the lighthouse lamp, and alert Prince Tamar in Falmouth. When the sleeping potion wears off, we will be left with a bunch of very angry ferrets and an even angrier wildcat. It could be very dangerous around here."

"I can go to Falmouth," announced Hannah. "I'm small enough to slip unnoticed past the guard post, and I know my way. I've been many times with Papa when he's selling his pickled herring."

"I know you could, my dear," said Hotchi. "But your old papa would never forgive himself if anything happened to you."

"Something will happen to me if I don't go, Papa, and to the beautiful Spatavian princess."

They knew she was right.

Penhaligon wrote a note to the crown prince, explaining that Porthleven was a town under siege and that Sir Derek was intending to rob him of his bride and her dowry. He found the coins in his pocket and pressed them into Hannah's paw. "When you've delivered this, find a decent meal and a safe place to stay."

Hannah whispered, "Take care of Papa, won't you? I worry about him."

"He'll be fine, I promise," said Penhaligon.

"Do you worry about your papa sometimes?" asked Hannah.

Penhaligon studied her worried face. He smiled and tweaked her nose. "I wasn't as lucky as you. I don't have a papa. Or a mama."

"But that's awful." The hoglet hugged him. "I don't know what I'd do without Mama and Papa."

Hotchi patted her on the head. "Come, lass," he said reluctantly. "I'll see you to the edge of town. We'll find Ma on the way."

Hannah, excited that at last she could really help,

kissed Penhaligon on the snout. "See you soon," she said.

Rowan and Penhaligon watched the hedgehogs scuttle down the alley.

"And I thought we had nothing in common," said Rowan.

"What do you mean?" asked Penhaligon.

"We're both orphans." Rowan peered anxiously up and down the alley. "So, who raised you?"

"Bancroft's mother," said Penhaligon. "Who are you looking for?"

"I'm surprised Donald and Dora aren't back." Rowan finally closed the door. "A badger family? That's unusual. You and Bancroft must be very close."

"Very." Penhaligon was uncomfortable with all the questions. "Don't you think we should concentrate on the night ahead rather than my private life?"

Rowan bristled. "Forgive me. I didn't realize it was such a sore subject."

"It's not a sore subject, just private." Penhaligon rummaged through his knapsack, unpacking his spare clothes. Eager to change the subject, he asked, "What did Hotchi mean about getting into trouble?"

Rowan picked up Penhaligon's clean britches and

measured them against her lower half. "He feels responsible for Bancroft's arrest. He went with him that night. He was supposed to distract the guard while Bancroft sneaked past."

"What happened?"

"Hotchi won't tell me. He just keeps saying it's his fault. Can I borrow these?" she asked, and, without waiting for an answer, slipped on the britches under her skirts. "I'll need a shirt too."

Penhaligon handed her a clean shirt, knowing there would be no use objecting. Rowan wasn't telling him everything, he felt sure. He knew he was right not to trust her.

The two foxes sat trying to ignore each other until the Hotchis arrived home with Old Amon.

Mrs. Hotchi-witchi wiped tears from her eyes. Hotchi had his paw on her shoulder. "There, there, Heli. Hannah's a brave and sensible hoglet. She'll be back afore you know."

"But she's just a wee little hoglet," sniffed Mrs. Hotchi-witchi.

Rowan sat her down and put the teakettle on to boil while Penhaligon explained their dilemma to Old Amon. The elderly goat pulled on his beard.

"Oh, aye," he said, nodding. "I've seen 'em building

a bonfire or some such thing on Brigand's Point, over-looking Sandy Cove. They be collecting a lot of wood from somewhere."

"That'll be it then, Mr. Penhaligon," said Hotchi. "They'll light a bonfire beacon on the point, and the ships will mistake it for the real lighthouse on this side of the bay. They won't have a chance. The ships will be sucked onto the shoals at Rock Pool Beach."

"Oh, aye," said Old Amon. "Be just like the old days. My grandfather was a beachcomber. He used to make his living on what were washed up from the wrecks."

"But won't the Spatavian ships know the difference between a bonfire beacon and a lighthouse?" asked Penhaligon.

"They'll be looking for a light, any light. I doubt any of those Spatavians have plotted this coast before." Amon dolefully shook his head as if the ships were already sunk to the bottom of the bay.

"We must destroy Sir Derek's beacon immediately," said Penhaligon.

"And make sure the real lighthouse is shining bright and true," added Rowan. "Old Amon, you worked the lamp once. Can you help us?"

"Oh, aye," said Amon.

# Ships Ahoy!

CHAPTER TWELVE

Before long, they had a plan. Old Amon would be smuggled into the lighthouse to watch for the Spatavian ships. When they were close, but not close enough to be in danger, he would light the lamp.

Hotchi-witchi, Penhaligon, and Rowan were to find and sabotage Sir Derek's beacon somehow, before the ferrets set it afire.

Hotchi gathered the supplies they would need. Old Amon watched and tugged his beard thoughtfully.

"So, ye comes from Ramble-on-the-Water, I hear," he said to Penhaligon.

"That's right," said Penhaligon.

"I have a cousin in Ramble-on-the-Water. Likes to bleat a lot. Don't s'pose you know 'im. His name's Bill Goat?"

Penhaligon rolled his eyes. "Oh, aye," he said.

🙋 🙋 🙋 🙋

There was no time for mistakes. It was past six bells, curfew time. If they met any of the guards now, it would be the end. No one spoke as the group hurried through the maze of alleyways until they reached the open path leading to the Rock Pool Beach lighthouse. Penhaligon was about to start up the path when Hotchi grabbed him.

"Watch out!" hissed Hotchi. "Guards!"

Sure enough, Penhaligon saw three ferrets strolling down the hill toward them.

"In here. Quick," said Old Amon, finding an open doorway.

They closed the door just as the ferrets came sauntering into the alleyway.

"Do we have to go this way?" one of them complained.

"It's the fastest way," replied another.

"Till you get us lost like you did yesterday," said the third.

"If you want to find any food left for supper, you'll stop whining and follow me."

The other two sighed and followed the first ferret

down the alley. "There better be some pickled onions left," they grumbled.

"Phew! That was close," said Penhaligon. "Come on, let's go."

The tall red-and-white lighthouse tower was finally in sight. They ducked behind a patch of spiky gorse bushes. There were two guards sitting at the base of the lighthouse. They appeared to be arguing over a card game.

Hotchi-witchi nudged Penhaligon. "I don't like the look of that," he whispered.

Penhaligon looked in the direction of Hotchi's paw. A rolling cloud of sea fog churned on the horizon.

"That fog will come in like pea soup. We'll hardly be able to see a thing. Them ships will see nothing at all," whispered Hotchi.

"Isn't there a foghorn in the lighthouse?" said Rowan, hitching up Penhaligon's spare britches and tightening the belt.

"Aye, there is," said Hotchi. "But Sir Derek's men would hear it too. Old Amon couldn't hold 'em off for long."

"Let's hope the ships get here before the fog," said Penhaligon.

"I would'nee bet on it," muttered Old Amon.

Penhaligon turned to Rowan. "Are you sure you can do this with your injured ankle?"

Rowan answered him with a scowl.

"Right. Hotchi, you first. Let's go."

Hotchi collected the items brought from his fishing box and crept, unseen, around the rear of the lighthouse and down the cliff path to Rock Pool Beach.

Rowan and Penhaligon marched directly up to the two guards.

"I hear you've been looking for us," said Penhaligon with a brazen smile.

The guards jumped up, surprised. Then they grinned at each other, letting their cards drop to the ground. There was a fat financial reward for catching the two foxes. Grabbing their weapons, they lurched at Rowan and Penhaligon.

The foxes sprinted to the cliff path. They hurried down toward the beach as fast as they could without losing their footing.

The ferrets were hot on their heels. "Halt!" they screeched.

Rowan and Penhaligon were halfway down and had scurried past Hotchi's hiding place. The hedgehog pulled tight the fishing line he'd strung across the path. The first guard tripped over it, and the second guard tripped over him. Over and over they tumbled until they landed in a heap at the bottom of the path. While they moaned and rubbed their bruises, Penhaligon cast a fishing net, gathering them up like Hotchi's herrings.

"That was easier than I thought," said Penhaligon. "Now for the next part."

Rowan and Penhaligon pulled off the protesting ferrets' uniforms and helmets and put them on.

Rowan winced. "When did you two ferrets last wash?" she asked.

Bound and gagged, the ferrets were dragged back up the cliff to a hidden spot behind the rocks.

"I wouldn't wriggle around," said Hotchi. "We brought you up 'ere 'cause the tide's coming in. I wouldn't want ye to fall back down there . . . unless you can swim?" The ferrets followed Hotchi's gaze to the beach below. They stopped wriggling immediately.

"Come on," said Rowan, sheathing her ferret sword. "Let's make sure Old Amon's in the lighthouse."

They found Amon looking out to sea with a telescope. He called down from the iron catwalk that encircled the lighthouse. "Ships ahoy! I think I see 'em. Two sets of sails. Way far out on the horizon."

"We must hurry; it'll be dusk soon," said Penhaligon. He clutched his spear. "And we don't know how many guards we may have to deal with on the way to Brigand's Point. Lock yourself in, Amon. And keep hidden."

"Oh, aye." He nodded.

Somehow Penhaligon knew this would be his reply.

Rowan scampered to the cliff edge. "What are you doing?" Penhaligon called impatiently. "There's no time for picking flowers."

She pulled up a patch of stringy white-flowered weeds and tore off the roots. Pushing past Penhaligon, she snapped, "Swallowwort."

Penhaligon hoped that Bancroft would still need the swallowwort. What if Sir Derek had already discovered him, sick and helpless?

♦ ♦ ♦ ♦

"Auntie, Auntie, what are you doing? You should be more careful next to that big hole. You could have fallen into the sea."

Lady Ferball turned to face her nephew, Sir Derek.

"I almost didn't recognize you in that ridiculous seaweed outfit. I think it was the tail that gave it away."

"Rats," said Lady Ferball.

"And what's this?" Sir Derek took the glass bottle, then looked at the kegs of ginger ale. "Tut-tut. You weren't trying to poison us, were you, Auntie?"

"You'll never get away with this, you scallywag," said Lady Ferball, shrugging his paw off her shoulder.

"Scallywag? Now there's a name I haven't heard since I was about six. It has a certain nautical ring to it, doesn't it? Like Jolly Roger."

"You pirate."

"Pirate? A pirate steals things. I don't intend to steal anything."

"I know you intend to steal the dowry from the Spatavian ships," said Lady Ferball.

"Auntie, you of all people should know that any items from the sea, or at the bottom of the sea, for that matter, are called salvage. And salvage, Auntie, belongs to whoever grabs it first."

"You . . . you . . . wrecker." The old cat was shaking with anger.

"Ah, yes. Now you'd know all about wreckers, wouldn't you, Auntie? You'd know because your great-grandfather was the most notorious wrecker on this coastline. You see, I remember all those stories you used to tell me when I was a little boy. I especially liked the tales about Cruel Coppinger and his cutthroats."

"Great-grandfather never forced a ship onto the rocks like Coppinger," said Lady Ferball.

"Of course not, not personally. He would just organize the villagers to help unload the cargo of any that had chanced upon a rocky fate. Such a helpful soul."

"Creatures were starving in those days. They had to make a living somehow."

"The Ferballs did pretty well, didn't they?" Sir

Derek gestured toward the manor, somewhere above. "I hated being sent here every summer when I was a kit, away from my family and my things."

"I always tried to make you welcome."

"Yes, yes, always the dutiful aunt. But I know you hated me, really."

"I didn't hate you, Derek. But you were, well . . . difficult."

Sir Derek didn't appear to be listening. "The rest of the family would be invited to the palace parties in the city, but never me. I know it was because I told Prince Tamar he had ears like a molting rat and a nose like a squashed parsnip. You'd think he'd be able to take a joke. He made such a stink and told his mommy. So I threw his crown into the moat. It was too big for him anyway."

"That was many years ago. You were both youngsters. Harming his bride and stealing her dowry won't make you feel better. Please, Derek," Lady Ferball pleaded.

Sir Derek smiled. "Yes, it will. Sorry, Auntie, I've made up my mind. It's not your fault. You always tried your best." Sir Derek heaved a pathetic sigh. "I couldn't help being a troubled youngster."

He led Lady Ferball away from the hole. "I have to lock you up in your room now."

She stopped in her tracks. "You can't."

"Of course I can," he said.

"No, I mean you can't lock me up there because . . . I want to be locked up down here."

"What are you talking about? You'd rather be in this cold, damp dungeon than your nice, warm bedroom? I think you really *have* lost your marbles."

"I insist."

"As you wish, Auntie dear." Sir Derek turned the keys in the cell door, locking his aunt in the dungeon. "I'll send someone to let you out tomorrow. Now, what did I come down here for? Oh yes. Keys. Well, as I don't need those anymore, I'll take your last jar of pickled onions instead."

"Oh, please, Derek. Not my last jar. Take pity on an old cat."

"My ferrets love your pickled onions, Auntie. You wouldn't deprive them of their last chance to enjoy them, would you?" He walked out with the jar tucked under his arm, almost bumping into Dredge. "There you are, Dredge. My aunt has decided to camp out in the dungeon for a while. As she's wearing a bunch of seaweed and little else, go to her room and find her a shawl. My mother would never forgive me if Auntie caught another chill."

He handed Dredge the spare key from the ring. "Oh, and you might want to inform your brave warrior ferrets that the terrifying sea witch that's been scaring them to death is in fact a real pussycat."

# A Barrel of Mischief

## CHAPTER THIRTEEN

The two guards on Porthleven Hill sat under the hedgerows, arguing.

"You said you were bringing it," said one ferret guard.

"I never did. I asked, 'Are you bringing it?' and you said yes," said the other.

"I said yes 'cause I thought you said, 'Shall I bring it?' and I said yes."

Hannah, hiding in the shadows, listened carefully.

"Well, you should go back and get it before I starve."

"Me go back? You should go back. You're the one who should have brought it in the first place."

"Right," said the first guard. "Let's toss for it before we faint from hunger."

"Go on, then," said the other guard.

Hannah crept closer, alongside the hedgerows. She heard a *ping* as a metal coin hit the lane.

"Drat! You dropped it," said the second guard.

"Help me look," said the first. As the two guards scrambled around on their paws and knees, Hannah seized her chance and scurried past.

Her progress was slow at first, creeping through the fields, keeping close to the tall bushes. At any hint of danger, she ducked into the undergrowth and rolled herself into a tight ball.

Soon she was on the main highway. She checked behind her to make sure no one was following, and even though she traveled as fast as her small paws could carry her, she knew she could be on the road for many hours to come.

The long shadows started to play eerie tricks. The little hoglet remembered the ghost stories her schoolmaster, Mr. Bancroft, would tell, late on an autumn's eve. It was almost autumn. The leaves rustled at her

as the breeze picked up. Her nose twitched. She could tell a fog was coming. She willed her chubby legs to carry her faster.

♀ ♀ ♀ ♀

The fog bank rolled in just as Amon had predicted. Rowan and Penhaligon argued as they clanked down the hill in their ferret armor, heading for the village. Hotchi puffed and panted, keeping up as best he could.

"I just meant it could be dangerous," said Penhaligon.

"So you expect me to sit at home and wait with Mrs. Hotchi-witchi?" Rowan's voice sounded tight with annoyance. "I wasn't raised to sit by the hearth."

"That's not what I meant. And I know how you were raised." Even as he spoke he regretted it. And doubly so when he saw the hurt flash through Rowan's eyes.

"So that's it. I suppose Lady Ferball told you about my Romany wolf mother. Well, I don't care what you think. I don't expect a pompous nincompoop like you to understand."

She strode off down the hill, leaving Penhaligon with his snout open once again. "But I didn't mean . . . ," he called after her.

Hotchi, who'd heard their conversation, patted the fox on the arm.

"Don't worry, Mr. Penhaligon. Rowan can take care of herself. She had a mighty 'ard time fitting in when she first came 'ere. Folk don't like what they don't understand, and that be the Romany wolves. Lady Ferball, she wouldn't put up with it. Said that anyone who upset Rowan upset her. Things settled down after that."

"What do you think, Hotchi? Are they the sly, savage creatures the stories tell about?"

"I can't say, sir. All I know is young Donald and Dora. They be a little wild, living in the woods most of the time, but nice youngsters. Hannah likes them a lot, and they keep an eye on my little ones. My youngest got herself lost one time. We searched for hours, and we almost gave up. Dora found her, fallen down an old mine shaft. They have good noses, do them wolves."

Penhaligon's own nose twitched as he smelled his ferret uniform. He sighed. "Let's catch up," he said. "If this fog becomes much thicker, our noses will be the only thing to do us any good."

They hurried after Rowan. Hotchi huffed and puffed, jogging to keep up with Penhaligon's long strides. "She's a proud one, Mr. Penhaligon. Don't take it personal."

"She called me a pompous nincompoop," said Penhaligon, wounded. "That's about as personal as one can get."

"She has a good heart, and she's real talented at the healing, you know. We all takes her advice when we're poorly. When Lady Ferball took her in, the poor thing were almost dead from cold and 'unger."

"I remember that winter," said Penhaligon. "I was assistant apothecary then. Many of our oldest and youngest suffered from the cold. Some even died," he added quietly. He thought of Menhenin and the portrait on the wall of his apothecary store. He wondered how Gertrude was getting on, if she'd been polishing the sign, if he would even see her again. Then he realized he'd only been gone for one day. He hadn't bargained for quite so much excitement.

Ahead, the fog had almost engulfed Rowan, hidden behind some wooden crates at the edge of the quayside. She had already surveyed the area.

"There are three guards at the checkpoint," she said. "Looks like the others have gone to the manor for their supper. I think we should pretend Hotchi is our prisoner and that we're taking him to Ferball Manor."

"Isn't that rather dangerous?" asked Penhaligon.

"Of course it's dangerous. But have you got any other ideas?"

Penhaligon shook his head. "Let's go." They pulled their helmet visors well down.

"All right, Hotchi," Rowan said in a deep voice, "you're under arrest." Before the hedgehog could object, the foxes grabbed him by the arms and frog-marched him toward the quay.

Their footsteps were muffled by the dank fog. It clung to everything it touched like wet tissue, and Penhaligon hoped it would aid their disguise. He could only just make out the Cat and Fiddle public house on the opposite side of the quay. They approached the checkpoint. Hotchi squeaked nervously.

Penhaligon's heart beat loudly in his ears. "Let me handle this," he whispered as they faced the three stern-looking guards.

"Who have you got there?" asked the largest ferret, poking Hotchi with the blunt end of his spear.

"I've been after this one for days," said Penhaligon. "His sniveling little offspring are forever hanging about and making mischief."

"You too?" said another ferret. "I made a catch meself

this afternoon." He turned to a herring barrel on the quayside and pried off the lid. "Look in there . . . a right barrel of mischief."

Rowan and Penhaligon peered inside. There, huddled

at the bottom of the barrel, snouts tightly bound and faces tearstained, were Dora and Donald.

"We reckon they've been thieving too," said another guard. "Look at this posh silk scarf we found. It was full of candy. Want one?"

Penhaligon's heart sank. "No thanks," he growled. "I have a bad tooth."

"We're just about to launch these two into the water," laughed the first guard. "We made some holes in the barrel, just a few so they sink nice and slow. Want to watch?"

Penhaligon saw a flash of panic in Rowan's eyes. His snout felt frozen. The guard yanked at Rowan's arm. "Come on, it'll be fun."

Penhaligon managed to blurt out, "Sir Derek needs to see this guard. He has important information about the sea witch."

The ferret took a step back. "You saw the witch?" he asked Rowan.

Rowan nodded her head vigorously.

"What did she do to you?" The ferret seemed very curious. He circled around Rowan and started sniffing.

Penhaligon knew the armor, although disguising Rowan's form, wouldn't completely disguise her scent. The ferret was seconds away from discovering Rowan's true identity.

"The guard cannot talk. The sea witch put a curse on his voice. Besides, Sir Derek is waiting for us."

The ferret stood aside. "Better hurry, then."

He'd done it. They were free to pass. He saw the tears well up in Rowan's brown eyes, and his heart sank. "Flaming foxgloves," he muttered to himself, and took a deep breath. "We'll take your prisoners too."

"What?" exclaimed the guard.

"Don't you remember Captain Dredge's orders? He said he was to interview every prisoner personally, in case they have important information."

The guard looked puzzled. "I don't remember that." He turned to his fellow guards. "Do you remember that?" The others shook their heads. The ferret looked at Penhaligon closely. "Come to mention it, I don't remember you either."

Penhaligon felt the heat of his stuffy helmet. He could barely think. "Er . . . you wouldn't. I've been at the hill checkpoint," he managed to blurt out. "Special duty." He tried to sound more casual. "Don't worry about those two, then." Penhaligon pointed at the barrel. "I'll just tell Captain Dredge you don't remember his order. I'm sure he'll understand." Penhaligon pushed Hotchi forward, and Rowan followed his lead.

They had gone a few paces when the guard called out, "Halt!" They froze.

The guard approached them slowly.

"I just remembered something about that order," he said. "So here, take 'em up to the manor for me." He pushed Dora and Donald, paws bound by a rope, at Penhaligon.

"Right," said Penhaligon, and pulled them sharply toward him. "C'mon, you two, we haven't got all night."

None dared to stop or speak until they were past the Cat and Fiddle and had taken the forked track that led to Sandy Cove.

"I never thought I'd be grateful that those ferrets on the beach smelled so bad," said Rowan at last.

She threw her head back and laughed. Her laughter was infectious. Penhaligon started to chuckle. Dora and Donald looked confused.

"It's me," she cried, "and Mr. Penhaligon." She gasped. "Please. Someone take this thing off my head."

Penhaligon helped Rowan to remove her helmet before he took off his own. Their sweaty fur stuck flat to their heads. Rowan self-consciously ran her claws over her head. Penhaligon had given up caring what he looked like.

She unbound the cubs. "That was quick thinking back there, Penhaligon." Rowan hugged the wolves. "I didn't think you had it in you. Thanks."

"Don't mention it." He sat on a rock.

Hotchi lay back and closed his eyes, trying to calm himself.

"Listen, Rowan. I'm sorry if I hurt your feelings," Penhaligon said. "I came to Porthleven expecting a few days' holiday at the seaside, and suddenly I'm in the middle of a siege, having to trust creatures I've only known for five minutes, some of whom I've been brought up to not trust."

"You mean wolves," said Rowan defensively.

Penhaligon sighed. "Yes, I mean wolves. I'm sorry. But I'm seeing things from a different side now. And I'm glad."

Rowan shrugged and almost smiled. "You can't help being a narrow-minded fuddy-duddy."

Donald and Dora climbed onto Penhaligon's lap and gave him a grateful squeeze. "Well, that's better than a pompous nincompoop, I suppose." He grinned.

Rowan laughed. Then she said, "I admit, I didn't trust you either. And I'm still not completely sure," she added.

Penhaligon snorted with indignation. Hotchi, eyes closed, grinned.

"We need to work together if we're to save those Spatavian ships," said Penhaligon.

Rowan nodded. "All right, truce?"

"Yes, truce."

"So, what's your plan when we reach the beacon?" Rowan asked. "There may be dozens of ferrets guarding it."

Penhaligon took a deep breath. "I don't actually have a plan as yet," he muttered. Rowan rolled her eyes. "We can't be certain that the sleeping potion will be taken by all the guards."

"Right," agreed Rowan. "So we should have a backup plan."

"Well, I noticed an abundance of dog rose in the woods by the manor. I'm sure you know that the rose hips make a very effective itching powder."

"So?" said Rowan.

"If the rose hips were to find their way into the ferrets' armor, it would soon make life very uncomfortable for them. It could create a useful diversion," said Penhaligon.

"Great idea, but we don't have time to mess about with dog roses. It will be dark soon."

"We don't, but Donald and Dora do."

"No. It's too dangerous," Rowan snapped.

Donald and Dora nodded excitedly and pulled at Rowan's arms, pleading.

"The ferrets take off their armor and leave it by the kitchen door," said Penhaligon. "We saw a huge pile when we left the manor, remember? If the cubs hurry, the ferrets will still be at supper. And with itching powder and the sleeping potion, perhaps we can put twice as many guards out of action."

Dora and Donald jumped up and down, Donald air-boxing with his fists.

Rowan had to laugh. "All right," she said. "But I don't like it. Now look, you two, only if there are no guards around and it is completely safe."

After many hugs and further instructions from Penhaligon on how to strip the itchy seeds from the rose hips, the cubs scampered back down the track toward the manor road.

Rowan watched until they were out of sight. "If they are caught again, I'll never forgive myself. Or you," she told Penhaligon.

"We're more likely to be caught standing 'ere, if you please," said Hotchi. "It'll be dark soon, and they'll be a-lightin' that beacon."

"Of course you're right, Hotchi," said Penhaligon. "We must press on."

The three trekked along the steep, narrow path

that cut into the cliffside. They were above the fog, which lay like a thick wad of cotton over Porthleven Bay. The path finally leveled off but was hard going, especially for the two foxes dressed in armor. When the path eventually descended into Sandy Cove, they would use the wooden steps next to Bancroft's boathouse to reach Brigand's Point.

Each creature was silent in thought. They knew how dangerous a mission this would be. Too many guards would mean their efforts would be in vain and their end uncertain.

Penhaligon's mind raced. What if he was wounded? What if Rowan was wounded? He quickly put the thought out of his head.

They hurried along in single file. Occasionally a rock hurtled from the path, disappearing into the hazy, crashing waves below, very far below. Penhaligon shivered. He felt the same way about heights as he did about small, dark spaces. He tried not to look over the edge.

Hotchi pointed out to sea. He danced up and down. "There they be." A pale outline of a sail showed through the dim light. "There they be. Looks like two of them. Clippers, I'd say, about five miles out. It's

hard to tell." He shook his head. "Them clippers fly fast through the water. If they be on a wrong headin', there'll be no turnin' back."

Suddenly a boulder, perhaps dislodged by Hotchi's excited antics, rolled down the path toward them. Rowan and Penhaligon jumped aside, but Hotchi was knocked down. His body curled into a prickly ball by instinct. He spiraled down the cliff path, then disappeared over the edge into the gloom.

Penhaligon and Rowan looked at each other in disbelief. They ran over to the edge, calling Hotchi's name.

There was no answer. Hotchi was gone.

"How do we tell Mrs. Hotchi-witchi?" asked Rowan, her voice aquiver.

"Hannah was counting on me. I made her a promise." Penhaligon covered his face as his eyes started to sting.

# The Great Escape

## CHAPTER FIFTEEN

Captain Dredge muttered to himself as he walked to Lady Ferball's bedroom, "I ain't no ruddy lady's maid."

Nevertheless, knowing that Sir Derek would see his aunt die of cold rather than be bothered to fetch a shawl himself, he strode into the room. She's not such a bad old cat, he thought. Can't help having a pompous tom for a nephew.

He looked around for some kind of blanket or shawl. There was a pile of clothes heaped on the bed. He went to grab a bed jacket and realized somebody was already wearing it. "What the . . . ?" He looked closely at the face under the nightcap.

"Not you again!" he roared.

🖋 🖋 🖋 🖋

Hannah had found a small stream from which to drink. She splashed the cool water onto her whiskers. She wasn't sure how much longer she could run along the hard road. Her paws were already blistered and sore. If she traveled across the fields, the grass would be soft, but she would be slowed down by having to climb the hedgerows that separated the fields.

Just then, she heard the rumbling of cart wheels. Above the rumbling she heard untuneful singing. "Nymphth and she-heh-pudth, come away, come away. . . ." The pig-boar farmer stopped his cart beside Hannah.

"Hello there. You be a pretty thmall hoglet out tho late on your own. You be lotht?" he asked kindly.

"No," said Hannah. "I have a message for the crown prince in Falmouth. It be very urgent."

"In that cathe, you better 'op up 'ere, my dear. I'll give ye a ride." The farmer helped Hannah into the cart beside him. "Gee-up there," he said, coaxing the horse into a trot. The farmer continued singing, and Hannah joined in, singing just as tunelessly as he did.

🕯 🕯 🕯 🕯

Donald and Dora had picked as many dog roses as they could carry and now sat in the greenhouse, scooping out the hairy seeds from the rose hips just as Penhaligon had told them. Before long they had a nice pile, which they tipped into little funnels made from rolled-up dock leaves. With the fog and the descending dusk, it was easy for the cubs to approach the pile of armor without being seen.

They soon had the job done. They used the funneled leaves like blowpipes; the damp seeds stuck nicely to the inside of the ferret armor and were too tiny to be noticed. They grinned mischievously at each other and scampered off to find somewhere to wash their paws.

🐾 🐾 🐾 🐾

"Gobbling goose grease," cried Lady Ferball. She had been picking unsuccessfully at the dungeon lock with a piece of sharp stone. "I'm a disgrace to the family." With a sigh, she sat on her seaweed skirts, which crinkled and crackled, being very dry. She'd never worn the costume so long without immersing it in seawater.

"Now what would Great-grandpa Ferball have done in a situation like this? He'd never have been caught in the first place, that's what."

She could see through the narrow slit in the dungeon wall that the light was fading. She peered through the keyhole to see if her nephew had left a guard. It was too dark to see anything.

Well, at least they haven't discovered Bancroft, she thought, for if they had, he'd have been thrown into the dungeon by now. Wait a minute, she thought. I should be able to see some light through the keyhole. She took another look.

With a smile, she broke off a large part of rubbery kelp from her skirt. Carefully, she spread it out flat and pushed it through the gap under the door, positioning it beneath the lock. Lady Ferball scrambled around on her knees until she found a twig that had been brought in with the straw.

"Derek hasn't changed a bit," she said. "He's still a lazy nincompoop." Holding her breath, she shoved the twig into the keyhole.

There was a jangling thud as the key chain, which had been left in the lock, dropped onto the seaweed. Lady Ferball gently pulled the seaweed toward her, but the bunch of keys was too thick to pass underneath the door.

"Rats," she said crossly. She shook the seaweed

gently time and time again until at last the keys settled flat enough for her to grab the end of a couple of
them. The rotted wood of the old door gave just
enough to allow her to pull through the keys.

She sorted through the ring of keys until she found
one for the dungeon door. It turned noiselessly in the
lock. Lady Ferball nudged open the door. She was
free.

The old cat hurried along the passage toward the
secret door. There were no guards. At this she wasn't
surprised. No one would think that a little old feline
could manage to escape from a locked dungeon. Lady
Ferball chuckled to herself.

There was a commotion coming from the great
hall. Instead of using the secret passage, she crept up
the spiral stairs. Peeking from behind the tapestry covering the stairway door, she saw dozens of ferret
guards.

The two rough-looking guards from the roof, Bert
and his friend Alfred, stood close. They had their
backs to her. She would have to be careful not to
make a sound.

Sir Derek stood halfway up the red-carpeted staircase with his wax-whiskered nose in the air. He was

wearing a suit of dark green velvet with a handsome breastplate of armor. He raised his paw to command silence.

"You have your assignments," Sir Derek yowled. "The Spatavian ships have been sighted. There's a sea fog hanging up and down the coast. Conditions couldn't be better. Those of you at Rock Pool Beach with Captain Dredge, do not start pulling wreckage out of the water until I arrive. Is that clear? Anyone caught doing so will be immediately and severely dealt with. Do I make myself clear?" he asked again.

There was a general murmuring among the ferrets. Sir Derek continued, "If any survivors make it to the shallows, do not bother to help them unless they are wearing something worth stealing, in which case help them to shore and then steal it. They should be so happy to be alive that they'll probably just hand it over to you anyway." There was a ripple of hacking across the audience.

Lady Ferball shook her head. She had warned her sister about being too soft on Derek when he was a kit. "Not enough attention and too much indulgence," she remembered saying. But as Lady Ferball didn't have any offspring of her own, her sister never took her advice.

"I am deeply disappointed that none of you has caught the foxes that have been on the run since this morning. Deeply disappointed," shouted Sir Derek, pounding his fist on the stair rail. His audience jumped.

Lady Ferball grinned. At least they haven't caught Penhaligon and Rowan, she thought.

"I would have hoped that two defenseless foxes would not be able to evade a whole army of ferrets. I want them caught and quickly. Otherwise, someone will pay." He dropped his voice to a seething hiss. "Do I make myself clear?" All the ferrets nodded enthusiastically. "I need just two of you to come with me to the bonfire beacon that we have worked so hard to build," continued Sir Derek.

Bert nudged his friend. "Hark who's talking. He never picked up a stick to help."

"We shall leave immediately to set it afire. And remember," he added, "as soon as the carts are loaded with the Spatavian treasure, we shall march to Penzance, where our ship awaits. Those of you guarding the manor and the village, pay attention. If you are not at the rendezvous, which is . . . ?"

"The-guard-post-on-the-hill," someone muttered in a singsong voice that was not altogether respectful.

"Yes, the guard post on the hill"—Sir Derek's feline eyes narrowed trying to spot the insolent ferret—"you'll be left behind. Warn the others that are not here." Sir Derek started down the stairs to a smattering of halfhearted applause.

Bert nudged his friend again. "Better make sure we don't fall asleep, then." He suddenly let out a loud belch. " 'Scuse me. Must have been them pickled onions." Bert yawned and stretched his arms. "You know, I am feeling rather sleepy. Probably too much dinner."

Lady Ferball smiled. The sleeping potion was working. Her heart leaped as someone shouted, "Hey! You!"

For a second she thought she'd been discovered. Then she realized her nephew was shouting at the two ferret guards.

"You two," yelled Derek. "Come with me. We'll march to Brigand's Point." Bert and his friend shuffled after Sir Derek. "And look lively." The two picked up pace to a quick march.

Just then, more shouts were heard, this time from upstairs.

"Let me go, you dunderhead. Why, I'll . . . just you wait, and I'll . . ." Bancroft was struggling to unlatch

himself from Captain Dredge's viselike grip. His cap
was covering one eye, and the bed jacket was bunched
up under his chin. Lady Ferball clutched the wall as
she felt her hind legs weaken.

"And what have we here?" asked Sir Derek.

"Found him snoring in your aunt's bed," growled Dredge.

"My, don't we look nice," said Sir Derek. Some of the ferret guard started to smirk. "Now, now, don't mock. He's just woken up, bless him." Sir Derek straightened Bancroft's lace cap, but somehow that made him look even more ridiculous. Soon the ferrets were uproarious; their hacking seemed uncontrollable.

Bancroft hung his proud badger head in shame.

Tears filled Lady Ferball's eyes.

# Voices in the Wind

## CHAPTER SIXTEEN

Sir Derek patted Bancroft on the back.

"Well, you turned up at just the right time. There's nothing like extra insurance at an important time like this. I have a feeling there's a certain fox around these parts who would be most interested to know that you are our guest once more. Of course he denied knowing you, but it's obvious you're all in this together. Hmmmm?" Sir Derek let out a dangerous-sounding purr and tickled the badger's chin with a sharp claw.

Bancroft said nothing, bowing his head so his eyes did not betray him.

"Dredge," snapped Sir Derek. "Lock him in the dungeon with Aunt Batty Catty."

Lady Ferball turned and ran back to the dungeon as fast as her skinny limbs would carry her.

Rowan put her paw on Penhaligon's shoulder. "It isn't your fault, Penhaligon. You've done the best you could."

"My best should have been better," he growled.

"Come on," Rowan said gently. "We agreed to carry on, whatever the cost." She wiped the tears from her eyes.

They trudged silently along the path, neither trusting their voice to speak without cracking. Penhaligon felt something deep in his chest, like a balloon about to burst. He couldn't contain it. He threw back his head, and a long howl whined from his throat. Rowan stared in surprise.

"I didn't know you could do that," she whispered.

"Neither did I," said Penhaligon, his voice hoarse. "But I know one thing: Sir Derek will pay dearly for the trouble he's brought to Porthleven. Let's go and take care of business."

"Wait." Rowan cocked her head to one side. "Listen." Her keen fox ears picked up a sound. "Do you hear that?"

Penhaligon strained his ears. "Very faint. What is it?"

"I can't quite make it out. This fog muffles everything. Listen."

They stood very still. Penhaligon heard his heart pounding in his ears but nothing else. Then a very weak voice cried . . . "H-e-l-p!"

They ran back to where Hotchi had tumbled off the edge. The call came again, stronger this time but still far away . . . "H-E-L-P!" Penhaligon lay on the ground and leaned out as far as he could while Rowan held on to his hind paws.

The black sea churned below. It seemed to call his name as it crashed against the rocks. "Pen . . . haali-gon," it boomed. The hackles on his neck rose up. He'd already escaped its watery clutches once. The fox knew that next time he likely wouldn't be so lucky.

"H-E-L-P!" There was the shout again. Through the gloom, Penhaligon saw a sight to make him forget his fears. Hotchi, spines all tangled in a twisted tree growing out of the cliff face, was holding on for his life.

"Hold on, Hotchi, we'll help you," shouted Penhaligon.

"I'm stuck, Mr. Penhaligon," he shouted. "My spines are caught in the branches."

"I'll climb down," said Penhaligon to Rowan, laying down his spear. "Give me your sword."

Rowan unsheathed the ferret sword and handed it to Penhaligon. "Be careful. I can't fight Sir Derek single-handed," she said.

He smiled, tucking the sword into the belt of his britches. Little by little, Penhaligon edged his way down, finding footholds in the craggy rock face. He slipped.

"Look out," cried Rowan.

He grabbed hold of the cliff face with the very tips of his claws. Gingerly, he continued his climb toward Hotchi. Just a few more feet and he'd be there. The cliff rock was slick and slippery. He wanted to climb

faster but knew that could mean answering the call of the sea far below.

"Hold on, Hotchi. I'm nearly there . . . ," said Penhaligon.

The ocean roared like some hungry monster. He felt dizzy. "Don't look down," he told himself.

On and on he climbed, trying to claw his way into the cliff so as not to slip again. He finally reached the tree, muscles shaking from the effort.

Hotchi's prickles had actually saved his life by catching in the branches. Untangling him would be more difficult. Penhaligon hacked away, pulling the branches from Hotchi's spines. The gnarled old tree groaned under their weight. The more branches Penhaligon cut, the less of a safety platform was left for the creatures to hold on to. The tree shook as the hedgehog trembled.

"Hotchi, you're going to shake us both out of this tree in a minute."

"I'm s-sorry, Mr. Penhaligon. I be that s-scared."

With a final splintering chop, Hotchi was free. "Mr. P-Penhaligon, sir, you be the b-bravest soul I know," he said, teeth chattering.

"You can thank me once we're back up there," said Penhaligon, pointing up the sheer cliff.

Fear worked well for the hedgehog. For all his bulk, Hotchi scaled up the cliff like a squirrel, stopping only when his short legs couldn't find an easy foothold. Penhaligon followed more slowly.

At the top, Hotchi grabbed hold of Rowan's outstretched paws. She dragged him safely onto the path. A shower of stones skidded from under Hotchi's scrambling feet. Down and silent they dropped until one of them struck Penhaligon hard in the face.

"Ouch!" Wincing in pain, he lost his hold on the rock. His claws scrambled. It was no use. Backward he tipped, farther and farther, toward the dark abyss below. He closed his eyes, his mind a confusing whirlwind. Now the Spatavians would be at the mercy of Sir Derek. Now Bancroft and Lady Ferball would surely be caught. Now he and Rowan . . . He prepared to suffer his fate as he fell.

Someone howled his name . . . "Penhaligon!" A screaming wind carried the name across the bay and with a gust pushed against his body. There he was, impossibly overbalanced, yet not falling.

"Hold on, Penhaligon," the wind whispered into his ears. His fur stood on end as though charged with static electricity.

"Menhenin?" gasped Penhaligon.

The wind did not answer but pushed him toward the cliff face. With more effort than he ever thought he could muster, Penhaligon threw himself against the rock and clung there. His chest heaved, and his heart beat wildly. "I'm all right," he spoke in a small voice. He wiped away the blood that dripped from his brow. "I'm still here."

The wind had disappeared.

He was suddenly aware of Rowan, crying out his name.

"I'm all right," he called back.

When at last he made it back to the cliff path, he was still trembling. Rowan flung her arms about him. Hotchi flung his arms about both of them.

"Ouch!" cried the two foxes.

# Beacon Afire

## CHAPTER SEVENTEEN

Penhaligon, Rowan, and Hotchi stood on Sandy Cove Beach. They couldn't believe their eyes. Penhaligon had thought it was a pile of driftwood, but the truth soon dawned on him. The spindled wooden skeleton before him was all that was left of Bancroft's beautiful boathouse.

"Oh, how could they?" gasped Rowan.

"They chopped it up good and proper." Hotchi sighed. "Must 'ave used it for the beacon."

They stepped carefully through the slashed paintings and books, dozens of them, torn and thrown carelessly in the sand. Penhaligon picked up a leather-bound copy he recognized. It was one he'd given to Bancroft as a gift when he'd left Ramble-on-the-Water.

Rowan pieced together some china and looked helplessly at Penhaligon. "His teapot" was all she could utter.

Penhaligon felt a rage brewing fit to burst his chest. He was determined that Sir Derek would answer for this. Pulling off his armor and grabbing his spear, he marched toward the steps that led up to Brigand's Point. Rowan followed until Hotchi called her back.

"Miss Rowan," said Hotchi. "They didn't find his boat."

Rowan saw Bancroft's rowboat, hidden under the sand grass.

"Let's see if it's damaged," she said. They pulled the vessel out from its hiding place. "It looks all right. We could use this if we have to. Come on." Rowan dropped her own armor in a heap on the sand. "Let's catch up with Penhaligon before he does something we'll regret."

🌿 🌿 🌿 🌿

Sir Derek soon realized that he had selected the wrong ferrets to undertake a very important task.

"You two must be the most dim-witted idiots in my entire army," he screamed at Bert and Alfred when they admitted they'd forgotten to bring Sir Derek's tinderbox. "How do you suppose we are going to light the beacon with no means to make fire?"

"I thought you brought it," Bert hissed to Alfred.

"You said you would bring it," Alfred snapped back.

"Enough!" commanded Sir Derek. "You!" He pointed his whip at Bert. "Go back to the manor immediately. Tell Captain Dredge to send me guards who know what they're doing. If there are any mistakes"—Sir Derek's eyes narrowed to two golden slits—"I shall put both of you on the bonfire when I light it."

The two ferrets trembled. Bert sped off toward Ferball Manor.

"It's almost dusk. Your friend had better hurry."

From his hiding place behind a pile of extra wood, Penhaligon watched Sir Derek and the guard as they stood before the smashed boards of Bancroft's home.

Sir Derek held a telescope to his eye and looked out to sea. "I can see them," he shouted. "If your friend isn't here with the tinderbox soon, your mothers will never see you again."

"I haven't seen my mother since Micklemas," sniffed Alfred. "Does it have to be *your* tinderbox, gov, or would this one do?" Alfred reached under his armor and pulled out his own little tin box.

Sir Derek smacked his forehead in frustration. "Get over there," he said, pointing to the pile of spare wood. "Find something to make a torch, AND LIGHT THE BEACON!"

Penhaligon seized his chance. With a snarling howl, he sprang.

Caught off guard, Sir Derek almost fell over. "So, you finally found the guts to show up." Sir Derek lashed out with his whip.

Penhaligon swiftly ducked but dropped his spear.

"Guard!" yelled Sir Derek. "Get that beacon lit now. I'll deal with this little problem myself."

Penhaligon dove at Sir Derek's legs. This time the

cat landed in an ungainly heap on the ground. In a flash he was on his paws. Hackles raised, he glared at Penhaligon.

"I don't think he'll be helping you tonight, Sir Derek."

Derek looked over to see Alfred sitting against the woodpile. He was holding a smoldering torch and was fast asleep.

"Looks like he overindulged on Lady Ferball's ginger ale," said Penhaligon.

"You don't think we'd be stupid enough to fall for that old trap! My aunt was caught red-handed trying to poison us. Your ridiculous plan didn't work." Sir Derek unsheathed his sword. "I touched nothing, and my guards ate only the pickled onions."

"Pickled onions?" repeated Penhaligon with a grin. "Your aunt is a step ahead of both of us, then."

Sir Derek lashed out with his sword. The blade caught the fox across his chest, slicing his clothes. Penhaligon clutched at the shallow, stinging wound.

"You'll pay for your meddling," shouted Sir Derek.

"And you'll pay for this waistcoat," Penhaligon shouted back.

He searched desperately for something with which to defend himself. Sir Derek thrust again with his sword. Jumping backward, Penhaligon narrowly avoided the point of shining steel.

Sir Derek laughed. "Your waistcoat will be hair ribbons by the time I've finished. And so will you."

Again he thrust. Again Penhaligon dodged the blade. He seized a plank from the bonfire. He whipped around; Sir Derek backed away. Penhaligon dropped the wood and ran to the sleeping ferret. Grabbing Alfred's sword, he turned as Sir Derek was upon him.

*Clang!* Sir Derek's sword crashed down, missing Penhaligon but landing with a loud ring on Alfred's head.

"Lucky for him he's wearing a helmet," said Penhaligon. "He needs it with your rotten aim." The fox readied himself for the fight.

They thrust and parried back and forth. Penhaligon made up for his lack of experience by dodging and jumping until they were both breathless. Round and round the bonfire they went. The steel swords chinked and clanked as they fought.

"You'll never win, you amateur," wheezed Sir Derek. "You're competing with years of good breeding and great swordsmanship."

"Is that right?" Penhaligon panted. "Heard your

father was a bit of an alley cat. Doesn't sound like much breeding to me."

"Why, you insolent scum." Sir Derek nicked Penhaligon's ear. The fox yelped in pain. "Shame you won't be around to see us raze Porthleven to the ground before we leave." Sir Derek lunged forward.

"I wouldn't count on it," roared Penhaligon, and he leaped on top of Sir Derek and pinned him to the ground, sword at his throat.

"Not bad for a country bumpkin fox," gasped Sir Derek. "But there's something you should know before you do anything hasty."

"And what might that be, pray?"

"If Captain Dredge cannot see the flames from the bonfire beacon before the clock tower strikes eight bells, you can say good-bye to your friend the badger." Penhaligon loosened his grip just a smidge. Sir Derek smiled. "You know, I don't think he'd be so lucky second time down the hole, do you?"

Penhaligon growled and pressed down with the sword.

"Ah-ah-ah," Sir Derek managed to choke out. "Also, if I don't return, I expect Dredge could find an old cat to join him."

Penhaligon rolled off of the cat and onto his hind

legs. Sir Derek brushed the dust off his velvet pants and smoothed his waxed whiskers.

"I'm afraid you lose," he mocked.

A ghoulish tone echoed through the air. Low and hollow, it seeped through the fog in all directions. A beam of light flashed weakly through the fog.

"It's not over yet." Penhaligon scowled.

"Who's doing that?" demanded Sir Derek. "Who's sounding the foghorn?"

"Another part of our ridiculous plan," said Penhaligon.

Sir Derek ran over to his sleeping guard. He grabbed the torch that was now flaming nicely, and he thrust it into the bonfire. The old, bone-dry timbers of Bancroft's house burst into flames. Soon the sky was bright orange and yellow. The beacon could no doubt be seen for miles.

"You are finished," Derek snarled. "Listen! Hear them? My ferrets will be here in minutes. They take no prisoners. The prize will soon be mine." He ran off toward the manor.

Rowan and Hotchi hurried over to Penhaligon. "Are you all right?" asked Rowan. "You're wounded."

"Only my pride," said Penhaligon.

They watched, helpless, as the flames licked high

into the twilight. There were shouts in the dusk, beyond the glow of the bonfire.

"The ferrets," said Penhaligon. "We have to leave."

A loud boom echoed around the bay.

"Look," said Rowan, pointing to the sky.

The fog glowed red and then yellow, like a fireworks display.

"Distress flares," said Hotchi. "The ships be upon
the rocks."

"Then we're too late." Penhaligon sighed. "We've
failed."

The ferret shouts were coming closer. Soon they would be hopelessly outnumbered.

"We can't give up now," said Rowan. "We can row around the headland in Bancroft's boat. We'll pick up survivors from the Spatavian ships. At least some will be saved."

"We'll end up on the rocks like them we're trying to save," said Hotchi.

Penhaligon stroked his snout thoughtfully. "Hotchi, you must hide from the ferrets, then return to the village. Persuade the villagers to help. If they break free the fishing boats, they can help rescue survivors."

"I don't know whether they will," said Hotchi. "I don't know whether they can. Everyone is scared of the ferrets, and even if they weren't, they are weak from hunger and haven't the strength to fight."

"They must try. Tell them Sir Derek intends to destroy Porthleven as soon as he has the Spatavian treasure," said Penhaligon.

"S'pose it couldn't be no worse than hanging off a cliff," said Hotchi. "I'll hide in that there woodpile. It won't take long to get to the village from here."

"Hotchi, you're brilliant," said Rowan.

"Aye, and I best be quick an' all . . . here they come."

Hotchi scurried into the woodpile, and Penhaligon

lay a couple of long planks over him and dragged Alfred in front of those, propping him up with his arm in the air as if he were waving. Hotchi was completely hidden.

"Wait until they're good and close before we make a break for it," warned Penhaligon.

"Keep your claws crossed," answered Rowan.

They could now see ferret shapes coming toward them. There were dozens of them. They waved spears and swords in the air as they ran.

"Get ready," said Penhaligon. "Now!"

They ran to the wooden stairway. Down the damp, slippery steps, they hurried to Sandy Cove. The frenzied shouts were very loud now.

"Listen to them," panted Rowan. "They sound possessed. They'll tear us limb from limb."

They leaped the last steps, landing in the soft sand. "This way," shouted Rowan.

It was hard, running in the sand. Their hind legs ached, and they stumbled to the rowboat. The boat was heavy, and the water's edge seemed so far away.

"Penhaligon," cried Rowan. "They're on the steps. Hurry!"

The ferrets were wild with excitement. They shook their fists and were leaping down the steps three at a time. They would soon be upon the foxes.

"We're not going to make it," sobbed Rowan as they inched along.

"We're almost there," said Penhaligon. He hoped Rowan didn't notice the desperation in his voice.

The ferrets looked bloodthirsty and fierce as they swarmed the beach like angry bees.

# Can Ferrets Swim?

## CHAPTER EIGHTEEN

"**B**ancroft." Lady Ferball shook the badger by the shoulder.

"What? Where am I?" Bancroft sat bolt upright with his nightcap still askew. Lady Ferball couldn't help but smile. "How long have I been asleep?" he asked.

"Since Dredge threw you in here with me," she said. "How are you feeling?"

"Actually, a bit better, although my chest is still sore."

Lady Ferball felt his forehead. "Your fever has calmed."

Bancroft looked around at the gloomy stone walls. "How long have you been locked up in here?"

"Not too long. Derek caught me lacing the ginger ale. But"—she held up a key to the dungeon door—"he didn't bargain for a sneaky old cat such as myself. Are you well enough to walk?"

"I think so." Bancroft staggered to his feet. He took an unsteady path to the slit stone window. The sound of Amon's foghorn drifted in with the fog. "Good gracious!" he exclaimed. "I'd be mightily confused if I was on board a Spatavian ship tonight. Look."

Lady Ferball saw, to the right, the lighthouse beam, looming through the fog. On the left, from Brigand's Point, glowed Sir Derek's bonfire. It was hard to tell where the foghorn was coming from.

"I see what you mean," she said.

"Mind you, I doubt if the ships' captains can see either of the beacons in this fog," said Bancroft.

"We'll get a better look from the cliff. Come on." Lady Ferball unlocked the door, and they headed up the stone steps. "We'll use the secret passage to the bedroom. The ferrets would never think to guard the upstairs."

The bedroom was warm and snug, a welcome change from the freezing dungeon. But they stopped only to grab a cloak and shawl to protect against the chill night.

"I'll go first," said Bancroft.

They tiptoed down the hallway to the minstrels'

gallery that overlooked the great hall below. The ferrets that had been left to guard the house were sound asleep, sprawled up and down the great stair and littering the marble floor.

"How on earth . . . ?" asked Bancroft.

"Penhaligon's sleeping potion and my pickled onions," said Lady Ferball with a wink.

"Poor Penhaligon," said Bancroft. "I haven't had a chance to tell him of the papers I discovered."

"Don't you worry," said Lady Ferball. "When all the excitement's over, there'll be plenty of time." She daintily stepped over sleeping ferrets.

Outside, the night air was cool and smelled of the chestnut and copper beeches that lined the estate. The fog was beginning to clear. They headed down the driveway to the cliffs.

The full moon was up now, shining bright. Neither of them was prepared for the sight that was to be revealed. There, stranded high on the rocks at Rock Pool Beach, bathed in the light of her own maroon flares, was a Spatavian clipper.

"How simply awful," said Lady Ferball. "What are we to do?"

Just then, Hotchi came hurrying down the path from Brigand's Point. Breathless, he could hardly speak.

"Your ladyship. Thank goodness." He made a short, polite bow. "And Mr. Bancroft, sir. I never thought I'd see you again after, well, you know." He hung his head. "You are both in great danger. Sir Derek says he's going to throw you and Mr. Bancroft here down the sea hole."

"Oh, he is, is he?" said the old cat. "We'll see about that. Now what of our friends the foxes?"

Hotchi explained all that had happened and how Rowan and Penhaligon were rowing around the point to the wrecked Spatavian ship.

"That's if they've escaped the ferrets. I've never seen 'em so mad. And now I'm supposed to persuade the villagers to break the fishing boats free. They'll never listen to me. I'm just a scared old hedgehog."

"Of course they will, Hotchi," said Bancroft. "You're one of the most respected members of the village."

"I am?" said Hotchi.

"That's right," said Lady Ferball. "I've heard excellent things about your character said by many of the fishermen."

"You have?" said Hotchi, holding his chest a little higher. "But what about the night you was caught, Mr. Bancroft? No one would respect me if they knew what a coward I was."

"You did what any smart creature would have done, Hotchi. You ran. Sometimes it's better to run and live to fight another day. It would have been silly for us both to be caught, wouldn't it? How would you have been able to help Penhaligon if you'd been arrested with me?"

"I never looked at it that way," said Hotchi. "You're right, Mr. Bancroft. I'd best get going, then . . . got a job to do." And he scuttled off toward the village.

"And if we're to be thrown down the sea well again, we'd best keep out of sight," said Bancroft. "Speaking of out of sight . . . Donald, Dora," he called. "I'd know your scent anywhere. Come on out of the bushes."

The cubs crawled out from the undergrowth, grinning as usual.

"I'm not sure what mischief you've been up to," said Lady Ferball, giving them a hug. "But I'm sure my nephew will be worse off as a result."

The cubs' grins grew broader.

ᕯ ᕯ ᕯ ᕯ

"Pull!" screamed Rowan.

"I'm pulling, I'm pulling!" Sweat ran down Penhaligon's whiskers as he strained.

The foxes felt water around their paws at last.

All at once, the hull was afloat. Rowan scrambled into the boat and positioned the oars in the oarlocks. After a final shove, the craft was out deep enough to dip the oars. Penhaligon, his strength sapped, tried to heave himself into the boat. "I can't make it," he gasped.

"Oh yes you can," cried Rowan. She grabbed him by the scruff of the neck and yanked him into the boat.

The ferrets reached the water, screaming and jumping up and down.

"Can ferrets swim?" asked Rowan.

"I hope not," said Penhaligon.

Then the strangest thing happened. The ferrets threw down their weapons and started stripping off their armor, throwing it on the sand as though it were red hot. One after another, the ferrets plunged into the sea.

The foxes could hear "Ooooh! Aaaah!" as the ferrets rolled around in the cool water like sea otter pups at a picnic.

Penhaligon and Rowan turned to each other and burst out laughing. "Donald and Dora!" they both cried.

🌲 🌲 🌲 🌲

The farmer shook a sleeping Hannah gently by the shoulder. She gazed around at the bright lanterns that lined the busy Falmouth quayside. They were stopped outside an inn.

"The crown printh be thtaying 'ere, I wath told," he said.

"Thank you so much," said Hannah, sliding down from the cart. "And I won't forget your invitation to visit you and Mrs. Pigswiggin in Sheepwash."

The farmer waved as he drove his cart down the cobbled street.

With a deep breath, Hannah marched into the inn.

🐾 🐾 🐾 🐾

The sweat trickling down Penhaligon's brow mingled with the blood from his wounds. His fur was dark and matted, and he knew he looked worse than he ever had in his life. He also felt more alive than he ever had. It felt good.

Through the lifting fog, he could just make out the frothy water warning of rocks beneath the surface. It crossed his mind that they might row into the darkness and never return. The thought did not scare him. The fact that Rowan was with him somehow made it more bearable.

It was hard to judge how far they should row out to sea before being able to safely round Brigand's Point.

"Are you scared?" he asked.

"No," she answered. "My wolf mother, Mennah, taught me always to have hope for the future."

"I want to understand, Rowan, so forgive me for asking this. But the tales of Romany wolves I heard as a cub left me quaking in my bed. There were unanswered questions, rumors about my parents, terrible rumors. Bancroft's mother wouldn't talk about them; neither would my apothecary teacher, Menhenin. I supposed that the subject was just too terrible to talk about."

Rowan was quiet for a moment. "What kind of rumors?"

"Just silly stuff I was teased about at school."

"Tell me."

"Well, they used to say that my parents had been eaten by Romany wolves. But I'm sure that's not true," said Penhaligon. But he realized that probably he wasn't so sure even after all these years.

Rowan stopped rowing for a minute to touch Penhaligon's arm. "That's a terrible thing to say to a young cub. No wonder you resent them. Creatures can be so cruel with their words." She continued rowing.

"Romany wolves are traveling people," she told him. "They keep themselves to themselves. Most creatures don't know or want to understand them. That's how the stories started, I suppose. I'm not saying that they wouldn't steal a turnip or two when times got tough on the Moor. But I always found them to be kind and understanding, almost like they knew how you were feeling without you even saying anything."

"Menhenin was like that," said Penhaligon. He pulled hard at the oars. "You never told me why the cubs don't talk."

"We're not sure if they can," said Rowan. "Bancroft says it's probably from shock."

"Shock of what?" asked Penhaligon.

"Seeing their mother die of wolf fever and then being lost on the Moor for days, without any food or comfort. We think the rest of the tribe, such as it was, planned to find a new camp and then return for the sick family, only they never came back," said Rowan. "The cubs were abandoned."

Penhaligon felt a pang of guilt. He'd been so caught up in his own self-pity. He'd not given any thought to the fact that the cubs or even Rowan had had such an unhappy life.

"What happened to the rest of the tribe?"

"I never found out," she replied sadly. "My wolf mother died of that same fever, seasons before. She was the tribe's birthing wolf. I've known the cubs since I helped bring them into this world. We lived apart from the others, Mennah and I. The tribe would send for her when they needed her. They didn't much care for the fact that she took in a fox cub." Rowan smiled. "But they got used to me after a while."

Penhaligon noticed how her eyes lit up when she smiled. "Do you know what happened to your birth parents?" he asked.

"Only what Mennah told me. My father was killed in an accident in the forest. My mother tried to look after me, but she died of a broken heart."

"I'm so sorry," said Penhaligon. Then he added, "At least they didn't abandon you."

"Your parents abandoned you? Why?"

"I don't know . . . maybe because I look different from other foxes."

"In what way?" asked Rowan.

Penhaligon felt uncomfortably hot. He wasn't sure if it was the rowing or his embarrassing confessions. "You must have noticed."

Rowan stopped rowing and studied Penhaligon. "Noticed what?"

"My fur," Penhaligon almost hissed, "and my large ears."

This conversation was going way beyond where he wanted it to go.

"Your fur? What's wrong with it?"

Penhaligon rolled his eyes.

"Maybe it's tipped a little darker than most," said Rowan. "Not much of a reason to abandon you. I kind of like it, actually."

Penhaligon smiled to himself and repeated Rowan's words in his head. His mind was still wandering when he realized she was asking him a question.

"Well, do you?"

"Sorry, do I what?"

"Do you think the whole tribe could have died of wolf fever? It's a mystery why they never came back for the cubs. They would always take care of their own. A friend of Lady Ferball's found the cubs wandering. He knew that her ladyship had taken me into her household, so that is where he took them."

"It's possible," said Penhaligon. "I've not had any experience with wolf fever, not having attended any wolves. If it is very infectious, then it's possible that's what happened."

They rowed in silence, both caught up in their own memories, until they rounded the headland. Crashing waves bashed against the jagged rocks. The water churned, and the little boat swayed, captured by the strong current.

"Penhaligon," said Rowan. "The boat seems to be drifting toward the rocks."

# Princess Katrina

## CHAPTER NINETEEN

"Flaming foxgloves!" cried Penhaligon. "Row! Hard!"

The salty spray spat at them, soaking their fur.

"Harder . . . pull. . . ."

"It's too strong!" yelled Rowan. "We'll never make it."

They were being drawn closer and closer. In another moment they would be on the rocks, just as Hotchi had predicted.

Penhaligon noticed a rhythm, how each huge wave washed over the rocks, then fell, skimming backward over the surface of the next incoming wave.

"Turn the boat around," he yelled above the roaring water.

They managed to turn the stern to the rocks.

"When the next wave washes back from the rocks, pull in your oar," he told Rowan.

A wall of water tumbled toward them. Pulling up their oars, they surfed the wave, wrenching free of the ferocious current. The booming waves at Brigand's Point were behind them.

"That was too close." Rowan's voice quivered.

"Don't worry," said Penhaligon. "That was probably the worst part."

"Listen," said Rowan. "I can hear shouting."

Haunting cries echoed across the water.

"There! Upon Rock Pool head," shouted Penhaligon.

Across the harbor mouth they rowed, toward the foundered ship. The lighthouse was quiet now, no foghorn and no beam of light. Penhaligon hoped Old Amon was safe.

The clearing fog gave way to a mantle of brilliant stars. The moonlight painted the bay with liquid silver. The night was beautiful, except for the macabre sight of the wrecked Spatavian ship. She was at the mercy of the mighty headland waves; her masts were dislodged and crestfallen. The rocks had ripped out her hull, and each crushing wave further weakened the boards.

As they approached the rough water, Bancroft's rowboat rose with the swell and crashed down hard into the troughs. The two foxes clung to the oars as the waves tried to whip them out of their grasp.

The ship had grounded not too far from shore. There was much confusion and shouting as Spatavian sailors jumped from the decks. If they were strong swimmers, they might make it. Otherwise . . . Penhaligon shuddered. The hammering waves took the clipper apart, plank by plank.

"Oh, Penhaligon, look!" cried Rowan. "The other ship."

The second clipper had already run down her sails and steered a hard starboard tack in order to avoid the reef. Still the vessel sped toward the rocks. She showed no signs of slowing.

The foxes willed the craft to swing safely past without grounding or being capsized by the waves. Penhaligon's teeth were clenched so hard they hurt. "Come on, you can make it," he whispered.

An awful, grating, heart-stopping sound ripped through the night sky. The clipper's hull scraped against an underwater ledge. It was just a graze. She was safe.

"I think they made it," said Rowan.

Sure enough, the vessel made for safer waters out in the bay.

"There is Sir Derek," said Penhaligon, pointing to the beach. "Like a vulture waiting for the last breaths of its prey."

Sir Derek and his ferrets waited for the sea to wash up her stolen treasures from the foundered ship.

The foxes rowed as close as they dared to the clipper. By now, most of the crew had abandoned her. Standing alone at the stern was a young feline. Her white-furred face reflected the moonlight. She clung, terrified, to the ship's rail.

Penhaligon called to her. "Jump!"

"*¡Socorro, no se nadar!*" came the anguished reply.

"Can you speak Spatavian?" Penhaligon asked Rowan.

"No, but I would guess she's saying she can't swim," answered Rowan.

"We have two choices," said Penhaligon. "Either you jump in to help her and I'll steady the boat, or I'll jump in and you steady the boat."

Rowan looked sheepish. "It was something I always meant to learn," she said. "But I'm really nervous in the water."

Penhaligon burst out laughing. "You mean you can't swim?"

"What's so amusing?" Rowan flushed.

"I'm just relieved that there's something you can't do," he said.

He threw down his jacket and dove into the water, for once leaving Rowan with an open snout.

# Treasure at Last

## CHAPTER TWENTY

Penhaligon had learned to swim in the River Ramble when he was just a cub. The river currents were strong, but nothing like the surging strength of these waves. Still, he was a good swimmer, and he swam close as he could to the ship.

"Please, Princess. Jump. I will help you." He spat out a mouthful of water.

Penhaligon wasn't sure if the princess could even understand him.

A sudden look of determination spread over her face. She ripped off her heavy velvet skirts.

"I coming," she howled, and flung herself off the ship.

It was several seconds before she resurfaced, panting and spluttering. Penhaligon grabbed her by the paws and swam to Bancroft's boat. Rowan pulled the princess and then Penhaligon from the water.

"I, Princess K-Katrina, th-thank you," the princess managed to stammer.

"Penhaligon, look," said Rowan, pointing to the harbor entrance.

Sailing toward the wreck was a ghostly regatta of fishing boats. Their boards were black with tar, their paint peeling, and their sails rotting.

Hotchi was at the head of the Porthleven fishing fleet. The rescuers began to pluck the Spatavian sailors from the sea.

"I don't believe it!" said Penhaligon. "Hotchi did it."

Just then, a tremendous splitting sound came from within the ship. With a last shudder, the clipper broke into two. It was only a matter of time before Sir Derek collected what he came for.

Princess Katrina was shivering and looked ill.

"She's swallowed too much seawater," said Rowan.

"We'd best make for the beach," said Penhaligon. "We'll take her to Mrs. Hotchi-witchi's."

"But what about Sir Derek?"

"We'll land farther up the beach. He's so busy look-ing for treasure I'm hoping he won't notice us. If we don't get the princess warm and dry soon . . ."

Rowan nodded. She wrapped her blistered paw with a handkerchief and took up an oar.

♕ ♕ ♕ ♕

Indeed, Sir Derek seemed too preoccupied to notice the little rowboat. But he *had* seen Hotchi's convoy of boats. He shook his paw in the air.

"Who was supposed to be guarding those fishing boats? They'll pay for their incompetence."

An unfortunate ferret that happened to be too close received a cuff around the ear.

"You there! There's a whole bolt of gold brocade. Pick it up before the sand ruins it. And you," he started on another guard, "are you blind? Look at that crate of cheese." Sir Derek waded in to grab a sack of oranges bobbing in the surf.

Bancroft's boat swayed erratically as the foxes and Princess Katrina approached the onshore waves.

"The waves are much bigger here," said Rowan nervously.

"Larger than I thought," admitted Penhaligon. "But at least the guards can't see us."

"It's all right for you," said Rowan. "You can swim."

The princess held tight as the swell caught hold of the rowboat and the waves thundered onto the shore.

"We'll be fine. Just try to keep her steady," shouted

Penhaligon. "We'll surf in, just like we did before. Ready?"

The swell lifted them up and too soon hurtled them forward.

"I'm not ready," cried Rowan.

Her oar had slipped from its oarlock.

"You lied, Penhaligon. *This* is the worst part," she screamed.

The lip of the huge wave curled, flinging the small vessel up on its bow like a matchstick. The three of them were tossed to the mercy of the water.

Penhaligon felt the breaking wave slam down on him like a falling tree. He thought of Rowan's words, "It was something I always meant to learn." He fought to the surface and was promptly swallowed by another breaker. Each wave propelled him toward the shore, but the current carried him away from Rock Pool Beach. When finally the surf had finished with him and he could feel the sandy bottom, he struggled to his feet. He ran through the shallows.

"Rowan! Rowan! Answer me, Rowan."

He came across the upturned boat. Close by were the oars, snapped in half like kindling. But the vixen and the princess were nowhere to be seen.

🌲 🌲 🌲 🌲

Lady Ferball and Bancroft had not encountered any guards on their way to the Rock Pool headland. Those that they did see lay in snoring heaps.

"Seems like Penhaligon's potion worked very well," mused Lady Ferball.

"I wonder why odd pieces of ferret armor are strewn around the village," said Bancroft. "It appears their owners just dropped them and ran off." He kicked at a metal breastplate. "Donald? Dora? You both seem to be very amused. Do you know anything about this?" The cubs grinned.

At the quayside guard post, Donald and Dora jumped up and down with excitement. They ran over to some ferrets, sleeping like newborns, helmets by their sides. One of them was holding Lady Ferball's silk scarf.

The cubs filled the helmets with stinking fish-barrel water and then replaced them next to their owners. Dora took the scarf and returned it to Lady Ferball.

"Thank you, Dora," she said, grinning as broadly as the cubs.

"I wish I knew what was going on." Bancroft sighed.

When they reached the lighthouse, Bancroft and Lady Ferball peeked inside while Donald and Dora scampered ahead to the cliff to see what was happening on the beach.

"Amon?" they called up the winding staircase. There was no answer.

"Hotchi did say Old Amon was manning the lamp, didn't he?" asked Bancroft.

The old cat nodded. "Well, he's not here now," she said.

They were about to leave when they heard banging

and muffled bleating coming from a cupboard. Bancroft tried the door, but it was locked.

"Just a minute, just a minute," he called to whoever was inside. He found an old metal bar. Wedging it into the hasp of the lock, he wrenched open the door.

"Old Amon? What are you doing in there?" asked Bancroft.

"You're lucky we found you," Lady Ferball said.

Old Amon couldn't speak until Lady Ferball pulled the sackcloth from his mouth. "Oh, aye," said Amon.

While Bancroft untied his ropes, the goat told of how he could see that the Spatavian ships were lost in the fog and heading for the rocks. He'd had to sound the foghorn, as the lamp alone was not enough. Unfortunately, the ferrets also heard the foghorn and soon came running.

"I held 'em off as long as I could by stacking things against the door. But I ran out of things," he said sadly.

"You did a fine job," said Lady Ferball. "We'd better relight the lamp so there are no more accidents tonight."

"Oh, aye. Good idea."

🕯 🕯 🕯 🕯

Sir Derek grabbed a case of beeswax candles.

"Bah!" he hissed as he realized the contents. "Where are the jewels? Where is the gold?"

The cases he and his ferrets salvaged from the sea contained everything and anything that a young bride might take with her to a new home—except gold and jewels.

He kicked the sack of oranges, scattering them across the beach. It was then he noticed the two figures foundering in the shallows. His sharp eyes narrowed. Rowan, he recognized immediately. It took only seconds to work out the feline must be the beautiful princess Katrina.

Sir Derek purred with pleasure. "Treasure at last."

# Catch of the Day

Penhaligon searched in vain along the beach, scouring the dark waters for any sign of Rowan or Princess Katrina. Several times he'd run to what looked like someone washed up on the shore, only to find it was the moon casting shadows from the surrounding rocks.

"It was a stupid idea," he muttered to himself. "I should never have gone along with it." He felt as though his heart had been shut in a lead box.

He was nearing the cliff path when one of the shadows stepped in front of him.

"Going somewhere?" the shadow asked. It was Captain Dredge.

"Don't try to stop me, Dredge. I'm in no mood to show you any mercy." Penhaligon stood defiantly, his muscles tight, ready to spring.

"I won't stop you," said Dredge.

"You won't?" repeated Penhaligon. "Why not?"

Captain Dredge shrugged. "It's time for me and my ferrets to cut our losses. We work for those that pay. Sir Derek's been promising a big payoff for weeks now, gold and silver, jewels beyond our wildest dreams." Dredge spat and gestured to the scattered debris washed up along the beach. "Food and wine and bolts of cloth, hats and shoes and linen for sissy beds. Some fortune," he sneered. "We'll be sailing off to warmer climes, me and my lads, once we've collected all our sleeping beauties. Interestin' ploy, by the way." He saluted Penhaligon. "Maybe we'll meet again someday."

He started up the cliff path. One by one his ferret army followed, including two in their underwear who glared at Penhaligon.

"If you're looking for a certain vixen," Dredge called to Penhaligon, "she's about the only jewel that's washed up so far."

Penhaligon heard frightened shouts down by the water's edge. He saw Sir Derek pull Rowan and the princess roughly to their feet. The fox's heart soared. They were alive! Not safe, but alive.

Skulking from rock to rock, he crept up behind Sir Derek.

"Where is the treasure? The gold and the jewels?" Sir Derek demanded with the point of his sword.

"The dowry is on the other ship," Princess Katrina spoke quietly. "On this ship were my clothes and provisions."

"Tough luck," taunted Rowan. "You're even a failure as a wrecker."

Penhaligon laughed to himself, until he heard Sir Derek's next words.

"And you fail to amuse me," he sneered. "I will use the princess to increase my fortunes. I'm sure the crown prince will pay handsomely for her. As for you," he told Rowan, "you have tried my patience once too often. You will join your mistress down the sea hole. Come along."

Penhaligon felt a pebble hit him on the back. He turned sharply and saw Donald and Dora hidden in the rocks a few feet away. They beckoned to him. Keeping low, he crept over.

Donald was very excited and thrust a jumble of strings into Penhaligon's arms. They had found Hotchi's fishing net that had been used to capture the ferrets. Donald gestured toward Sir Derek.

"Smart thinking," whispered Penhaligon. "We'll

launch a surprise attack." The wolf cubs wriggled with excitement.

Sir Derek dragged Rowan and the princess up the beach.

"Stand on your own two paws," he shouted at the weak and stumbling princess Katrina. They started up the path. Again the princess fell to her knees.

"Get up," ordered Sir Derek.

"Can't you see she's ill, you mangy, moth-eaten moggy," screamed Rowan, aiming a kick at his shin.

Sir Derek's eyes blazed with rage. "How dare you," he spluttered. "No one speaks to me like that." He let go of the princess and lunged at Rowan.

"Then it's about time someone did." Rowan sank her teeth into his paw.

Sir Derek yowled in pain.

"Lady Ferball always said you were a spoiled cat."

At that moment, Penhaligon threw Hotchi's net and then leaped onto Sir Derek's back. The cat fell to the ground with Penhaligon on top of him. The more he struggled, the worse of a tangle he became. He blew and blustered and rolled around until even Princess Katrina couldn't help but smile.

"Captain Dredge," Sir Derek yelled. "I order you to

help me. There'll be an extra financial reward for anyone who'll help me!"

No one came. He hadn't noticed the ferrets leaving
one by one. He was all alone.

He glared at Penhaligon. "Where's my army?"

"The only army around here is that one," said Penhaligon, pointing up to the edge of the cliff, where
several dozen of the king's Warthog Army stood in a

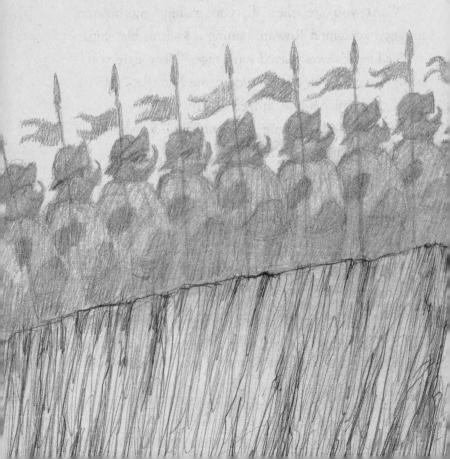

shadowy line. Little Hannah, holding Prince Tamar's paw, jumped up and down, waving.

"Well," Penhaligon told Rowan, standing with his hind leg on top of the trussed Sir Derek, "that seems to be wrapped up." He dusted down his soaking, filthy, torn clothes. "Do you know anywhere I could have my clothes pressed and a nice hot bath?" he asked.

# Secrets Revealed

Penhaligon's head nodded gently as he dozed in Lady Ferball's library. With a log fire in the grate and a full stomach, he was most content. It had been a hectic few days at the manor. Princess Katrina had been quite unwell after her near drowning, and Penhaligon and Rowan had been tending to her night and day.

Katrina and the crown prince had left that morning, both of them eternally grateful and promising great rewards to the foxes and all the brave villagers of Porthleven.

Lady Ferball had been bustling through the manor, directing her staff to clean everything and then clean it again. The ferrets had left the house in a terrible state, and there had been an awful smell about the place. But now the floors were clean, and the furniture smelled of beeswax. A delicious aroma of ginger wafted from the kitchen, where Lady Ferball had her sleeves rolled up, concocting her next brew.

The library door swung open with a crash. Penhaligon sprang out of his seat.

"What the . . . ? Rowan? What are you doing?"

He rushed to hold open the door as Rowan struggled in, balancing a tray.

"Now, Penhaligon, don't make a fuss. I have to check your wounds. We don't want them to go putrid, do we?"

She pushed Penhaligon backward into his chair and inspected the gash he'd received while saving Hotchi.

"Just as I thought. Abscess. You didn't clean this properly, did you?"

"Well, I haven't had the time. There's really no need for this. Ouch!"

Rowan trimmed the fur from around his forehead. He winced as she daubed an herbal salve on the cut. "What is that stuff? It smells awful."

"Can't tell you." Rowan smiled. "It's a secret, ancient family recipe. Stop squirming around." She took a razor from the tray.

"You aren't going to drain it, are you?" asked Penhaligon, horrified.

"Mm-hmm." She nodded. "Don't worry, you won't feel a thing."

Penhaligon squeezed his eyes shut, waiting for the sharp stick of the razor.

"Right, you can look now. I'm all finished," said Rowan.

"But I didn't feel a thing," he said.

"Told you." Rowan picked up the tray. "I have to find some extra dressings. You sit here and relax for a while."

"Rowan?" said Penhaligon as she reached for the door. "Er, would you like to go over some herbal tonic recipes later?"

Rowan's amber eyes flashed as she smiled. "I'd love to." She closed the door behind her.

Penhaligon settled down in his chair, a satisfied smile on his face. He dozed peacefully until the library door flew open a second time, with a louder bang. Once more the fox jumped out of his chair with a start.

"Lady Ferball?"

"Now don't get up, Penhaligon. You need to rest." She backed through the door with a pitcher, closely followed by Donald carrying a tankard and Dora a plate of homemade gingerbread.

"You have to try this ginger ale. I think it's the best batch I've ever made."

"You really shouldn't have—" started Penhaligon.

"Nonsense," she said. "You need to get your strength back, young fox." She placed it on the table next to his chair while Donald ceremoniously unfolded a napkin and laid it over Penhaligon's lap, then bowed.

Dora placed the gingerbread next to the pitcher, then curtsied. Both the cubs gave Penhaligon their usual toothy grin and then slammed the library door behind them.

Penhaligon took a sip. It was good. The ginger warmed within while the fire warmed without. His heavy lids drooped over his eyes, and his head nodded.

There was a bang as the library door flew rudely open once more. This time, Penhaligon spilled ginger ale all over his clean britches.

"What the . . . ? Bancroft? What are you doing?"

The badger was struggling with a large steamer trunk. Penhaligon hurried over to help.

"Thanks," said Bancroft, mopping his brow. "Perhaps we can finally have a chat about that very important news I had to tell you."

"Flaming foxgloves, I'd forgotten all about that," said Penhaligon. "After the goings-on of the last few days, nothing seems to be that important anymore."

"Oh, but it is," said Bancroft. "I think you'd better sit down."

He opened the trunk lid to reveal reams of documents, a few old paintings, clothes, and other mementos. Blowing dust off a faded piece of parchment, he handed it to Penhaligon. The fox unrolled the letter and read.

*My dearest Mrs. Brock,*

*With a heavy heart, I leave my cub, Penhaligon, in your valued care. We have pleaded with his grandfather, but he will have nothing to do with foxes.*

*Our voyage to the New Land will be long and treacherous. I pray we will return safely in the spring. Until then, I know Penhaligon will be safe with you. His mother has placed a lock of her fur and mine in a silver clasp; even as I write, it is still damp from her tears.*

*You are a true and loyal badger and the only one that ever understood. My wife is lucky to have you for a friend. No one in Ramble-on-the-Water knows our secret. It must be kept that way for the sake of our cubling son, Penhaligon.*

*Until we meet again,*

*Mawgan*

Bancroft handed Penhaligon a silver locket. The fox opened it and touched the soft amber fur of his mother and the coarse jet-black fur of his father.

"It's so . . . unusual for fox fur," he whispered. He swallowed hard.

"It's not fox fur, Penhaligon," said Bancroft gently. "Your father was a wolf. A Romany wolf."

Penhaligon's throat went suddenly dry. He could hear his heart pounding in his ears. "I don't understand."

"I found this trunk amongst Mother's belongings after she died. It was hidden. I don't know if she'd forgotten about it or whether she had thought it best not to tell you. It's not the kind of thing that's easy to tell."

Everything Penhaligon had known was suddenly in a whirl, and yet it almost made sense. The part of the puzzle that was missing had finally turned up. He wasn't sure if he was ready for it.

Bancroft sifted through the papers. "There's more." He handed another letter to Penhaligon.

*My dear son, Mawgan,*

*I pleaded with you to give up this vixen. Foxes bring nothing but bad luck. You see what hardship it brings to my sister, Mennah, who'd rather live as an outcast than to give up her orphan fox cub.*

*You ignored my advice and look where the two*

*of you are . . . scorned by both races. The way of the
Romany wolves is best. We live amongst our own in
our own tribe.*

*I refuse to take care of your cub while you and
your fox wife seek the new life you desire, but only so
you'll reconsider this madness.*

*You fool yourself, Mawgan. There will be no
quiet life for you, even in the New Land. Let us talk.
Don't leave with anger in your heart.*

*Your father,*
*Menhenin*

Penhaligon was stunned. "Menhenin? My Menhenin?"

Bancroft nodded.

"If Menhenin was my father's father, then that
means he was my *grandfather*?" He stared at the letter
in disbelief. "Menhenin was a *wolf*?"

Bancroft patted him on the shoulder. "Yes. A wolf
and brother to Rowan's wolf mother. I would say the
two of you have much in common, my friend."

Penhaligon's head was spinning. There was too
much to take in.

"He fooled all of us for years," Bancroft continued. "It must have been hard for him not to tell you. He left his tribe to live amongst the villagers and help you find your way. He must have loved you very much."

"I never considered why he was so kind to me." Penhaligon sat, bewildered. "If only he'd told me, I could have . . ."

"You could have what? He knew what kind of a reputation Romany wolves have. Penhaligon, you couldn't have loved him more, and he didn't want to take the chance that you'd love him less."

Bancroft unfolded a worn letter that had been handled many times. "This was from Mother to you." He handed it to Penhaligon.

Penhaligon read Mrs. Brock's letter in silence. She wrote of how his parents had asked her, his mother's best friend since childhood, to look after him when he was a tiny cub. The arduous journey would have been too much for one so young to survive.

"They was planning to be back by the next season," she wrote, "but fate was crueler than the cold sea that took them." She explained how much it broke their hearts to leave him and how she'd promised to care for him as she would one of her own. "And I loves ye as much as my Bancroft, you pair of rascals," ended the letter.

Penhaligon wiped a tear from his eye. "Dear Mrs. Brock. She knew the whole story. No wonder she always encouraged me to spend time with Menhenin."

"I expect Menhenin felt the grief as much as you. Mawgan was his only son."

Penhaligon suddenly laughed. "The silly old coot, wearing those robes all the time to disguise the fact that he was a wolf."

"I think it was ingenious," said Bancroft. "If the villagers of Ramble-on-the-Water had known there had been a Romany wolf in their midst for all those seasons, and their apothecary too, they'd be outraged and hysterical." He added quietly, "And you would have become an outcast."

Penhaligon's laughter turned to tears. And he cried until there were no more tears left in him.

"Your parents never abandoned you, my brother." Bancroft hugged Penhaligon. "They were taken while searching for a better life where they wouldn't be judged so harshly."

Bancroft's nose started to twitch and wrinkle.

"It must be a shock, finding out about your father," he said slowly, sniffing indelicately around Penhaligon's head. "You seem to be taking it much better than I'd thought, knowing how you feel about Romany wolves and all that. Phew! I say, Penhaligon. This probably isn't the time to bring it up, but have you had that wound on your head looked at? It smells awful."

Just then, Rowan entered the room with the clean

bandages. She hummed as she gently dressed Penhaligon's wound.

Penhaligon smiled. "Actually, Bancroft, Rowan tended to it already. The smell is the salve she used."

"What the devil is it made from?" asked Bancroft.

Penhaligon looked down at his dark-tipped fur. He held his paw out to Rowan. "I can't tell you. It's a secret, ancient family recipe. My family."

# Epilogue

A public holiday was declared when Crown Prince Tamar and Princess Katrina bestowed the honor of knighthood on the newlyweds Sir Penhaligon and Lady Rowan Brush.

Villagers from all over the west gathered to celebrate, and Penhaligon and Rowan's friends were guests of honor at the Ferball Manor banquet.

Old Amon conducted a splendid fireworks show from the lighthouse while Cuthbert Ramsbottom, having arrived with several barrels of his famous Warren Arms blackberry ale, conducted the singing. The mouse, accompanied by a cart full of giggling nephews and nieces, spent much of his time trying to persuade Farmer Pigswiggin and his wife, from Sheepwash, that one rendering of "Nymphs and Shepherds" was enough.

🌲 🌲 🌲 🌲

Many seasons passed, and all remained quiet in the village of Porthleven. Old Amon's beard grew so long he sometimes tripped over it on his way to wind the clock in the tower. Lady Ferball also was living out her seasons. All of Porthleven mourned the day she died peacefully in her powder-blue bedroom.

Her spirit was long remembered.

Sir Penhaligon and Lady Rowan felt her determination as they nursed their patients at Ferball Manor Hospital. Bancroft heard her laughter each time he rang the morning bell in the new schoolhouse and library. Hotchi caught her strength when reeling in the nets of his new fishing boat, while Hannah, who'd been Lady Ferball's constant companion, was the keeper of her wisdom and wonderful recipes.

Gertrude was now in charge of Ramble-on-the-Water's apothecary. She had been quick to inform Penhaligon that the mark on the brass sign had come right off when she'd applied a little banana juice and sea salt.

As for Sir Derek, well, he had a longish stay in the palace dungeon, but eventually Crown Prince Tamar allowed him to leave. He was family after all, the prince had said, however distant. No one had seen him since.

There was, however, a rumor passed on by a fisherman that a black-and-tan cat had been sighted swabbing the decks of a sailing ship in some foreign port. The master of the ship was a burly ferret by the name of Captain Dredge.

But no one really thought of Sir Derek anymore, except the children of Porthleven when they begged Donald and Dora (who began speaking soon after Rowan and Penhaligon adopted them) to tell them of the daring adventures of Penhaligon Brush.

🕯 🕯 🕯 🕯

Penhaligon rubbed at the brass sign on the hospital door. It read:

IN LOVING MEMORY OF
LADY FERBALL

Satisfied, he threw his cloth at the polish tin. He looked out to sea, where the fishing fleet was busy with the day's catch, and then to the horizon beyond. He sighed.

"My goodness," said Rowan. "That was a big sigh."

"Oh hello! I didn't see you there."

"Anything wrong, Penhaligon?" she asked.

"No, everything's right," he said, giving her a peck on the cheek. "But it's been very quiet around here lately, hasn't it?"

"Donald and Dora are at school."

"No, I mean, for a while now. It's just that we're still young foxes, aren't we? We can travel, have a little excitement?"

Rowan raised an eyebrow, but then a slow smile crept across her face. "Okay, but this time, I want my own britches."

## THE END

Here's a special preview of
Penhaligon Brush's next daring adventure,

# The Curse of the Romany Wolves

Excerpt copyright © 2009 by S. Jones Rogan.
Published by Alfred A. Knopf Books for Young Readers, an imprint of Random House
Children's Books, a division of Random House, Inc., New York.

# The Curse

It was Rowan, with her fox's sharp sense of smell, who had discovered the pustule-like swellings behind Donald's hairy ears. The cub was lying on the crisp white hospital bed-sheets, staring at nothing, with a dead creature's eyes. His long, dark fur was wet from the sweat of fever.

Rowan took Penhaligon aside. "I've seen this before," she said in what was almost a whisper. "The high fever, the unblinking stare, the stinking, putrid swellings . . . they start behind the ear. . . ."

Penhaligon nodded. He too recognized this illness. He also knew that soon the poison-filled swellings would cover Donald's paws. But that would not be the worst. It was the pustules they could not see that were the most dangerous, the ones inside his body. Penhaligon dreaded Rowan's next words, but knew he had to listen.

"These are symptoms of the sickness that wiped out the Romany wolves so many seasons ago. I shall never forget that terrible time of despair. We nursed so many, Mennah and I, until she too . . ." Rowan's voice trailed off. She swallowed hard. "You must have seen it, Penhaligon, when Menhenin was ill; he was from the same Purple Moor tribe. It's the Curse. The Curse of the Romany Wolves."

The words echoed around Penhaligon's head. It couldn't be possible. The devastating disease had died out with the wolves. Donald and Dora were the only survivors, and they had always been as healthy as herring gulls.

Penhaligon felt a veil of sadness wrap around his body as he recalled the illness of his grandfather and apothecary teacher, Menhenin. Penhaligon had not been able to save him, though he had attended the old wolf night and day, to the point of exhaustion. No cure had helped. Menhenin himself had been strangely calm, accepting, almost as though he knew his fate.

"Yes, I have seen it," Penhaligon said quietly, "though I did not know at the time what the sickness was."

"How could you have guessed? Menhenin kept his wolf identity secret. You would not have suspected a sickness that affected only wolves. Besides," she added, "there was nothing you could have done. Mennah and I tried everything—studied ancient family cures over and over, until she fell to the sickness herself. Penhaligon, what are we to do?"

He heard the panic in her voice and hoped she couldn't detect the same in his. "Try not to worry. We'll find a cure." He placed his paws around her.

"You know as well as I, Penhaligon: this is wolf fever; there *is* no cure."

Was she right? They *had* all died: Menhenin; his sister wolf, Mennah; the Romany wolves from the moor. Some of the desperate tribe had left, but had never been heard from again. Donald and Dora had been spared. But had wolf fever now returned to claim the ones it had left behind?

They heard singing and turned to see Dora sitting on Donald's bed, holding his paw.

"Dora!" Rowan barked. "Get away from him right now!"

"But I want to see Donald. What's wrong with him, and what's that stinky smell?"

Rowan snatched Donald's paw away from her. "Leave this minute!"

"Why are you shouting at me?" Dora shouted back. "I want to know what's wrong."

"Don't come back until I say so!" Rowan pointed to the door.

Dora's snout quivered with anger. "I hate you!" she growled, and ran from the ward.

Penhaligon watched Rowan's eyes well with tears. "There is no cure for wolf fever," she said again.

"Rowan, I won't give up till we discover one." He hoped his words sounded more confident than he was feeling. "Why don't you rest? We have a long night ahead. I'll watch Donald for a while."

Rowan gave a heavy sigh. "I can't rest, Penhaligon. And we haven't even talked about what will happen if this news gets out. The rumors, the fear and prejudice toward the wolves . . . What about Dora? And you? Remember how long I was an outcast in this village—a vixen, raised by a Romany wolf?"

"Now, Rowan, you worry too much. Creatures have moved on since all that superstitious nonsense. Everyone loves and respects you and the cubs. So what if Mennah was a wolf? Because of her, you are a talented healer. What's more, through both you and me, the villagers have had benefits from ancient wolf knowledge that they would never have had otherwise. They know there is nothing to fear."

Bill Goat had been watching and listening from his bed at the other end of the ward. He stroked his white beard thoughtfully. "So . . . the Curse of the Romany Wolves returns. Well, good luck to you, Penhaligon," he mumbled as he heaved himself out of his comfy bed and grabbed his walking stick. It was time for him to leave.

🕯 🕯 🕯 🕯

The wind-driven rain chittered against the windows. Penhaligon set down his apothecary book in order to draw the curtains. He had studied dozens of books and his candle had burned down to within a bare inch of the holder, but still he could find nothing regarding wolf fever. It was as though the disease had never existed. How could the books written by great apothecaries of the past fail to mention such a terrible disease? Had the wolves really been so hated that other creatures had simply ignored the illness? He pressed his paws against his aching eyes.

He should check on Donald. Lighting a fresh candle, he started down the sweeping red-carpeted staircase of Ferball Manor. He paused in front of a portrait in a large gold frame. Lady Ferball's feline emerald eyes smiled upon him. The artist had captured the old cat's lively spirit so well that Penhaligon felt he could almost reach out and touch her. "Dear Lady Ferball, how I wish you were here with us right now," he said quietly.

Once downstairs, he crossed the black-and-white-marbled entrance foyer to the hospital ward. The room had once been the manor's grand ballroom, and the ceiling was painted with colorful scenes from Ferball family history: tall ships and castles and royal-looking felines captured forever in oil paint. Sometimes Penhaligon would lie on one of the hospital beds just to gaze and imagine.

But now he had eyes only for Rowan and Donald. The vixen sewed as she sang softly to the still, staring cub. She smiled, but Penhaligon could see the rims of her eyes, stung pink from tears.

"I've given Donald an infusion of feverfew tea and have poulticed the swellings behind his ears with bog mud and oat grass." Rowan pointed to the thick layers of brown gunk behind his ears. "He seems more comfortable, but his eyes are so dry from the staring. I bathed them with nettle juice." She tried to sound matter-of-fact, but the edges of her snout trembled a little.

"He knows you're taking the very best care of him," said Penhaligon gently. "What are you sewing?"

Rowan held up a dark blue tunic. She was working on the scarlet embroidery around the neck. "It's Donald's costume . . . for the festival. I feel I must finish it, even though . . ." Her voice trailed off.

"We'll find a cure, Rowan. There must be a cure. Its just a matter of knowing where to look and what to look for." Penhaligon waved his paw in front of Donald's eyes; they did not even flicker. "Are there any signs of swellings on his paws?" he asked.

"Not yet," said Rowan.

"I remember Menhenin's sickness. . . . After the paw swellings, his fever broke. He felt much better for a while."

"Yes. But then the swellings burst," said Rowan, "and the cough comes." She stabbed the needle into the tunic and fiercely drew the red thread through the fabric.

Both foxes knew that this was when the poison spread inside the body. After that, it would only be a short time before the infected creature lost the battle with wolf fever.

"How did Donald catch such a disease?" asked Rowan.

Penhaligon shook his head. He had been puzzling over the same question. "Has he been anywhere unusual recently? Perhaps he came in contact with something tainted by wolf fever?"

Rowan shrugged. "Not that I know of, but you know they only confess to half their mischief." She smiled and stroked Donald's brow.

"I wonder if they sneaked down the old tin mine again." Penhaligon felt the tips of Donald's ears. "You know how fascinated they are with those damp old tunnels. Goodness knows why." He felt chilled just thinking about the cramped, dark mine. "We need to speak to Dora; they are always together."

Rowan thought for a minute. "That's true, except for the time I sent him to the cliffs at Rock Pool. We needed more snake-egg shells for Bill Goat's stomachache cure."

Penhaligon sighed. "Well, unless he met a stray infected wolf over there, I can't see that Rock Pool would be a problem." He scratched his head. "Menhenin taught me that sometimes a disease can live in a creature for a long time, but might only make that creature sick when the disease becomes stronger than its victim."

"Donald? Weak?" Rowan stroked Donald's paw and hummed the sweet yet melancholy melody she had previously been singing.

The tune stirred a sudden swelling of emotion inside Penhaligon. He wasn't sure if it was a feeling of sadness or hope. "That song . . . I recognize it. Menhenin used to sing it sometimes when he was working in the apothecary in Ramble-on-the-Water."

"It's a Romany wolf song," said Rowan, "a lullaby to soothe aching hearts. It's strange, I hadn't thought of it in a dozen seasons. Mennah sang it to me when I was a cub." She rested her head against Penhaligon's arm. "My heart aches so much, I think that it's breaking."

Penhaligon jumped up with a start. "Flaming foxgloves! Why didn't I think of it before?"

"Whatever's the matter?"

"Menhenin . . . the attic . . . the old apothecary shop. There was a trunk up there, stuffed full of his old things. There were some ancient apothecary books. I can't find any reference to wolf fever in my books, but I bet I would in those. I hope Gertrude didn't throw them away."

"But I thought you'd brought all Menhenin's old books with you to Porthleven?"

"Only the ones we used in the apothecary. The ones in his trunk he never used—'out of date,' he always told me. It's just a hunch, but, Rowan, don't you see? All those seasons ago, Menhenin wanted to keep his identity as a Romany wolf hidden. It stands to reason that he would hide any books that described the afflictions of Romany wolves."

Rowan looked puzzled.

"Wolf fever strikes what kind of creature?"

"Well, wolves, of course."

"Exactly. And Menhenin knew that if I found his fever symptoms in an apothecary book, I would discover that he was a wolf, not a fox, underneath all those flowing robes and turbans he wore."

For the first time since Donald had become sick, Penhaligon saw a spark of hope in Rowan's eyes.

"Oh, I do hope you're right. I mean, there must be a record of a cure somewhere. . . . Oh my gosh! Old books!" Rowan suddenly dropped her embroidery.

"Rowan, what is it?"

"I'd forgotten all about it." Rowan eyes sparkled with excitement.

"Flaming foxgloves! What?"

"Well, Mennah used to speak of an ancient book of cures that had been used by the Romany wolves for generations. The book was lost, or maybe stolen, she thought, at around the time Menhenin left the tribe. When wolf fever appeared, she begged the elders to search for the book. She felt sure they'd discover a record of the cure for it. But the sickness spread so quickly that the book was never found."

Penhaligon studied her for a long moment. "And you think the book may be in Menhenin's trunk? You think he stole it?"

"No . . . I . . . . Yes, it's possible. Not 'stole' it; maybe borrowed it. Would it not make sense that he'd want to teach his grandson as much Romany wolf medicine as he could?"

The question niggling its way into the forefront of Penhaligon's brain finally jumped out of his mouth. "Rowan, if Menhenin knew of a cure for wolf fever, then why didn't he use it when the Romany wolves on the Purple Moor were dying? Why didn't he heal himself?"

Rowan sighed. "You just said yourself, Penhaligon, that perhaps he didn't want to give up his secret identity."

"I don't believe that Menhenin would let the whole of his tribe die if he had the cure. It's a preposterous thought." Penhaligon felt frustration bubble up inside him.

"Perhaps he became too sick too quickly to think reasonably. But there's only one way to find out. You must go to Ramble-on-the-Water," said Rowan.

Penhaligon looked at Donald, and his frustration turned into determination. He took Rowan by the shoulders. "If you are right about the book, then I promise I will find it. And if it contains the cure, I shall concoct it. Am I not a renowned apothecary?" He pecked her on the cheek. "Just make sure that costume is finished in time. Donald will need it for the festival. I'll leave for Ramble-on-the-Water at first light."

Rowan rolled her eyes. "Let's hope you can make it through the doorway, now that your head is so big. You shouldn't make promises you may not be able to keep."

Penhaligon laughed. It was good to have her teasing him again. He would say anything to keep the despair from her eyes. "So I see we finally got rid of Bill Goat," he said.

Rowan noticed Bill's empty bed for the first time. "Why, the old goat didn't even say good-bye." Her snout suddenly dropped. "Oh no! Penhaligon, you don't suppose he heard?"

"There was never anything wrong with his hearing," said Penhaligon.

"That's all we need." Rowan grimaced.